Peppermint and Pentacles

THE RED CAPE SOCIETY, BOOK 3

MELANIE KARSAK

CLOCKPUNK PRESS

Peppermint and Pentacles
A Red Riding Hood Retelling
The Red Cape Society, Book 3
Copyright © 2017, 2018 Clockpunk Press
All rights reserved. No part of this book may be used or reproduced without permission from the author.
This is a work of fiction. References to historical people, organizations, events, places, and establishments are the product of the author's imagination or are used fictitiously. Any resemblance to living persons is purely coincidental.
Published by Clockpunk Press
Editing by Becky Stephens Editing
Proofreading by Rare Bird Editing

Created with Vellum

For Erhan

Peppermint and Pentacles

CHAPTER 1
The Most Wonderful Time

The clock on Tinker's Tower gonged out nine o'clock as I slipped down the cobblestone street, turning into a narrow alley. A flurry of snowflakes carried by a stiff winter's breeze blew down the passage and up under my cloak. I shivered and pulled the garment closer around me. Yawning tiredly, I paused to ensure I had not been followed, then entered through a nondescript door.

Inside, Marcus stood guarding the second door, one hand on his pistol, the other holding a cup of tea. The scents of anise and orange filled the small alcove.

I smothered a laugh when he trained his gun on me while taking a sip.

He lowered his teacup. "You're late, Clem," he told me with a smirk.

"Suppose they'll kick me out of the Society?"

"You wish," he said with a laugh.

I chuckled.

Setting the tea down, he unlocked the door and motioned for me to enter. "Good luck."

I huffed a laugh and headed inside. The room within appeared to be a humble abode. The small flat had a cot, a rough-cut wood kitchen table, and a cold hearth. The place was perfect in its depiction of misery and meanness. I crossed the room to the worn wooden cupboard. I eyed the old wooden pantry. The initials R. M. were rudely carved at the top. I opened the cupboard door. On one side was a row of shelves sparsely lined with chipped teacups, empty tea tins, and plates. On the other side was a drum of potatoes. I slipped around the barrel then slid the panel on the back of the pantry open to reveal a narrow set of stairs leading below the city. I entered the tight stairwell, closing the panel behind me, and then descended. I could already hear voices rising from behind the closed door at the bottom of the stairs.

Wonderful.

I really was late.

I wound down the stairs, pausing just outside the door. Orange light poured through the cracks around the doorframe. And with it, warmth. I rubbed my hands together, my fingers numb from cold, then opened the door.

Heat and light poured from the room.

They were gathered at a long wooden table; its cherry wood glimmered with so much polish, reflecting the golden light cast by the chandelier overhead, that it hurt my good eye. I winced. Every agent sitting at the table turned and looked up at me.

Agent Hunter was already passing out dossiers as he went over the weekly report. He gave me the briefest of glances.

"Clemeny, good of you to join us," he said.

I slipped into my seat. "A bit early for someone on my beat."

"Yes. Well, we all have challenges," he replied.

I looked around the table. Half the other agents were rolling their eyes or frowning at me. Unfriendly bunch. The other half looked on with sympathy. Friendly enough. And a few others—Pippa, Cressida, and Hank—smirked and passed me knowing glances. Friends.

I scanned the room for Harper. She wasn't there. From what I'd heard, she'd rotated off Cressida's beat and was working on a case about which everyone was very hush-hush. Whatever it was, I hoped for Harper's sake that it included a trip to Africa. It had been months since we'd worked the *Fenrir* job, and I had yet to be assigned a new partner. Surprising even myself, I was starting to miss that redhead.

Agent Hunter cleared his throat. "As I was saying, of primary concern at this moment is the continued fallout from the death of the Queen of Hearts. An operator calling herself the Red Queen—not very creative, is she?—is making moves to fill that vacuum. Her Majesty has asked for additional agents on this case. I have assured her the Red Cape Society has everything under control. Therefore, we must act quickly. Atticus, you and Cressida will join George and Claire on the case," he said, setting dossiers in front of both of them.

"Thank you, sir," Atticus said with a nod.

Cressida slid the dossier toward herself with one finger. "Sir, I don't mean to protest, but I'm making headway in recovering the artifact in question in my current assignment. This is not the best time to set that operation aside. I have traced the mirror to—"

"I understand," Agent Hunter said. "But I need you on this case."

"Yes, sir," Cress replied with a frown.

"Now, can I have everyone's attention? We have enhanced our protocol for significant event reporting and requests for funds. Please direct your attention to the board, where I have outlined the new, basic procedure," he said, motioning to a chalkboard so full of notes that it looked more white than black. The unfriendly crowd pulled out small leather journals and notepads and began attentively taking notes as Agent Hunter continued. Some of the friendly-enough crowd were kind enough to pay attention. Cress, doing a poor job of hiding her annoyance with being reassigned, sneered with frustration and looked toward the fireplace across the room. Hank checked his pocketwatch. Pippa flipped through the dossier in front of her then leaned back with an exasperated huff.

As I glanced around the table, I made two other observations. First, everyone else had tea and scones. I did not. And second, everyone else had a leather dossier in front of them. Again, I did not. The second issue was a non-issue. With the full moon coming, I had plenty of work. In the last few months, contenders had been popping up, testing Lionheart's resolve. Since he'd been reluctant to be bothered with them, I'd been stamping out all the fires. There was enough going wrong to keep me busy, and I most certainly didn't need a new case. The first issue, however, required immediate remedy.

I rose and went to the sideboard. Taking a small plate, I selected the last nut and date scone. I grabbed a cup and saucer. Slightly miscalculating the size of the saucer—a common problem since I'd lost sight in my left eye—I nearly lost my cup, making the china clatter.

The loud noise earned me a reproachful cough from Agent Hunter.

"Sorry," I mouthed wordlessly.

Moving more gracefully, I poured my tea, adding a dab of honey and a slice of lemon. I stirred in the honey as I listened to Agent Hunter.

"If you require additional funds for your current mission, you must detail that information, with all amounts listed and totaled, in triplicate…" *And on, and on, and on.* As I stirred, I eyed Agent Hunter.

I'd heard that he engaged in boxing at the Society's gymnasium, and his form was undoubtedly that of a pugilist. Even in his perfectly tailored suit, I could see the flex of his bicep muscles. His yellow hair was neatly trimmed, the mutton chops on his face well-groomed. I fancied he smelled of cinnamon, and not for the first time, I imagined he tasted the same.

The truth was, since the *Fenrir* case, Agent Hunter was never far from my mind. I'd spent more time at my desk at headquarters in the last few months than I had the four years prior. Agent Hunter…intrigued me. I lifted my teacup and sipped, hiding the smirk that lit up my face. Unbuttoning that piece of work would be like unwrapping a Christmas package. Who knew what gifts were underneath? I imagined the tastes of cinnamon and the salty tang of sweat.

"Any questions?" Agent Hunter asked. He scanned the room. When his eyes met mine, his perfectly formal expression faltered for a moment, and the corner of his mouth twitched as he suppressed a smile. He glanced away.

To my astonishment, a hint of blush rose to his cheeks.

Hell's bells, had my thoughts been so apparent on my face? Trying not to chuckle—or run screaming from the room in terror—I took my tea and scone and sat back down.

Hunger overcame humiliation, and soon I was lost to my breakfast while some of the others asked for the finer details on meal expense limitations. The conversation droned on endlessly. It was only when Hank perked up with a question did I find something in which to be interested.

"Should we be expecting a holiday bonus this year?" Hank asked.

It was four days until Christmas. Last year, Her Majesty had seen fit to gift us all with a little extra coin as thanks for risking our lives to deal with the deadliest, ugliest supernatural elements in her realm. It had hardly seemed thanks enough. This year's bonus was late in coming.

"Unfortunately, there was no budget in the coffers for it this year. But if you visit Master Pennington's butcher shop in Covent Garden, you will be supplied with a Christmas goose at no cost. Simply inform Master Pennington to charge Mister Grey."

This time there was an audible groan of disappointment from the entire crowd.

Agent Hunter sighed. "I know, I know. I do commiserate. I will be enjoying my Christmas goose in lieu of a bonus as well," he said then rolled his eyes.

I grinned at him.

To my surprise, he met my eyes and gave me a soft smile.

"Now, you all have your assignments. Please review them. I don't anticipate any issues, but you may contact my office if you have any concerns," he said then turned to Cressida who had already opened her mouth to protest once more. "Once the situation with this Red Queen is attended to, we'll return you to your regular case."

Frustrated, Cressida grabbed her dossier and bag then rose, her red cape swirling around her, and left in an angry huff.

I leaned back in my seat to finish off my tea before heading back outside into the cold winter air. Yawning once more, I scanned the table. No dossier. No change in assignment. Good. No one could do what I did anyway.

All the others had just departed when I finally took the last sip. Setting my cup down, I pushed my seat back then rose to go.

"Agent Louvel," Agent Hunter called, crossing the room to meet me. "You don't have your dossier. I was hoping to discuss your case with you before the meeting began, but since you were late—"

"Yeah, late night. Sorry, sir."

"Yes. Indeed. In which case, I think you will appreciate this temporary reassignment," he said as he handed a leather folder to me.

"Temporary reassignment?" I asked. I stared down at the binder. Deliciously button-down or no, Agent Hunter could not possibly think that taking me off my beat so close to the full moon was a good idea. And there was no way another agent was going to get Lionheart to cooperate.

"Her Majesty asked for you by name on this one."

"Did she? Why?"

Agent Hunter shrugged in such a manner that indicated he knew why but was not saying.

I took the brief from his hand then sat back down. Agent Hunter sat beside me, waiting patiently as I scanned the pages.

The intel on the case was minimal, but it seemed that children had been disappearing from homes and charity schools all along the Strand not far from St. Clement Danes…the church where I had been abandoned as a baby, and the neighborhood in which I'd grown up.

Ah. Now, just how did Her Majesty know enough about me to make that connection?

"Not much here," I said, choking down some stray emotions that wanted to bubble to the surface.

"No, that's why we need you on the case."

"You do know the full moon is coming."

"Yes, that's why you'd better get this situation resolved before your regular duties come howling," he said with a soft chuckle.

"Was that a joke?" I asked, raising an eyebrow at him. I smiled softly.

"It was an attempt," he said, shifting nervously in his seat. He tried to suppress a smile, but this time, he was less successful. His left cheek dimpled in the most adorable manner. It took everything inside me to ignore the image of him and me lunging onto the well-polished table, the silver buttons on his coat popping off like fireworks, the taste of cinnamon and salt tingling on my tongue.

I coughed, clearing my mind. "It was a good one," I said, casting him a sidelong glance. Why wasn't he married? Certainly, there wasn't any shortage of girls out there looking for a well-employed man with good manners, a solid build, and a soft smile.

"Right. Well. Very well then," he said, standing, returning to his rigid posture and manner once more. "Do you need anything for the case?"

I sighed. *Dream on, Clemeny. There is no way this man is ever going to see you as anything but just another agent. He probably has some elegant lady in the country embroidering his face onto a pillow and dancing the quadrille with him at a country ball.*

"No…not yet. I'll go have a look, check in when I

can. I will need to keep an eye on the wolves as well. I'll be pulling double duty, you know. Suppose that will earn me two geese?"

"I'll see what I can do," he said then held my chair as I rose, pulling it back for me.

I stuffed the parcel inside my satchel, gave Agent Hunter an appropriate and formal nod, then headed toward the door.

"Be careful out there, Clemeny," Agent Hunter called. The comment was benign, but there was a lilt to his voice, an edge of genuine concern that caught my attention. And he'd called me by my Christian name.

"Thank you, sir," I said, hoping he didn't hear the catch in my own voice. I headed back outside to the cold London streets.

Or…just maybe…

CHAPTER 2
Oranges and Lemons

St. Clement Danes. Why my mother—whomever she was—had chosen to leave me on the doorstep of that particular church in London, I would never know for sure. Maybe the reason had something to do with Saint Clement being merciful. Perhaps she hoped God would take mercy on her for leaving an hours-old baby in a basket on the church steps. Or maybe she hoped Saint Clement would be merciful to me, or that I would stay on a sound and Godly path since she'd delivered me—literally—to God's doorstep. I had no idea. But what I did know was that I would be forever grateful for the church organist, Widow Louvel, who'd taken me in and raised me as her own.

As I headed back across town, snowflakes started to fall. It really was Christmastime. I had hardly given the holiday a second thought. My work for the Red Cape Society had me far busier than I realized. Picking off stray wolves and quelling arguments had become commonplace jobs. In truth, I had been both busy and lonely. Quinn was back on his feet but still very much retired, and Harper was gone. It was just the wolves and me. Even Lionheart had grown strangely quiet. I hadn't seen him in weeks. No wonder I was spending so much time at headquarters ogling Agent Hunter. But now, my boots were headed back home for the first time in longer than I cared to admit.

I stopped by the bakery where I picked up a loaf of bread and some gingerbread cookies and then at the grocer to get a bottle of claret. Well stocked, I headed to Grand-mère's house.

Widow Louvel lived in a small flat just off the Strand near Saint Clement Danes. I headed up two flights of stairs until I reached the door. Inside, I heard the woman whom I'd come to love like she were my own flesh and blood singing in her native French.

I knocked on the door. "*Bonjour,* Grand-mère."

The singing stopped, and a moment later, the door opened wide. "Clemeny, oh Clemeny, oh Clemeny, oh Clemeny, oranges and lemons, come in, girl," she said, hugging me so tightly that I could barely breathe. "Good lord, you're skin and bones. Come inside."

Grinning, I entered behind her, then closed and

locked the door. I took a moment to check the locks. I had additional security installed on her flat after the incident with Fenton. I doubted anyone would ever try to bother my grand-mère again, but just in case. After all, wolves had uncanny noses and sharp minds when it came to hunting for advantage against their enemies. Fenton had gambled and lost. But still.

"I was just thinking about you this morning. I will go to the chocolatier and get some good French chocolate—even Belgium is okay, just not this English sawdust—and make us a Bûche de Noël for Christmas. And what do you want? Oysters? Ham? You know, I hate that disgusting English plum pudding, but you like it, so I can make some and choke it down just so you can have it, if you want. But you need to eat. Clemeny! Oranges and lemons. You're too thin. I don't like this work you are doing. You're not eating. Please, tell me you have found a man. Have you? And what is this?" she asked, looking at my bags.

Chuckling, I handed her the parcels. "Claret, bread, and cookies," I said.

"No cheese?"

"I forgot."

"It's no matter. I have some Brie cheese—not much mind you—but I will go today and get us some nice Camembert. When will you be coming for Christmas? Why don't you come stay with me? Your room at

Missus Coleridge's is too cold. Unless you have a man wooing you. Then you must attend to that. Sit, sit," she said, leading me to a seat at the table.

She sat down across from me then and looked pointedly at me, lowering her reading spectacles to the bridge of her nose. Her sharp blue eyes looked piercingly at me. "Tell me about this man. Who is he? Tell your grand-mère."

Unbidden, the image of Agent Hunter in his perfectly tailored suit crossed my mind. "A colleague at work," I blurted out, hoping to end this line of questioning.

Grand-mère nodded. "So, Eliza kept her world then. Mmmm," she mused, pursing her lips so tightly together it looked like it hurt.

Every night, I hunted werewolves, chased them across the rooftops of London while firing silver bullets and wielding a silver blade. I never felt rattled. But sitting here, under Grand-mère's steely gaze, my hands started to shake, and my heart slammed in my chest.

"Very well," she said, her eyes softening, her lips reforming into a smile. "Bring him here. I will decide." She patted my hands. "Now, I will make some tea and prepare us something to eat, and you will tell me why you are here."

I exhaled deeply.

Grand-mère chuckled, her back turned to me.

"What have you heard about the disappearances? Two children from Saint Clement's Orphanage? Then, another boy, Tobias Brown. And a girl, from further down the Strand, Emily Stratton."

"Oh, yes. That's big news around here. All the parents have the children practically locked in the house like prisoners, especially after what happened to Harry Alperstein."

Harry Alperstein? Digging in my bag, I pulled out the dossier and looked through my notes. There was no mention of Harry Alperstein. Thus far, there had been four abductions, but Harry was not on the list.

"And who is Harry Alperstein?"

"Harry Alperstein is the bank clerk's son. He was abducted from a locked room without a window right under his parents' noses. The Bow Street Runners have been looking into it, but nothing so far. Clemeny, are you on this case? Is that why you're here? They don't think those werewol—"

"No, I don't think so."

"Thank goodness," she exclaimed, her hand to her heart. "It's bad enough thinking someone abducted those children, but to think it might have been those… creatures. That's more than a person can handle."

"True," I said.

"The Browns' flat is just up the Strand. Their child was the first to go missing. You should start with them.

And Pastor Rosenberry will see you, I'm sure," she said as she set a plate in front of me. Her voice did not sound so confident. Pastor Rosenberry, who was there when I'd been discovered that cold morning twenty-five years ago, had never cared for me.

I looked down at the plate. Freshly baked bread, Camembert, sliced apple, thin-sliced salted ham, and a handful of nuts.

My heart warmed, I smiled at my grand-mère. "*Merci*," I told her softly.

"*De rien*," she replied, pinching my cheek.

Pushing her own plate aside, set her elbows on the table, and leaned in. "Now, tell me more about this man."

CHAPTER 3
Tidings of Comfort

S omeone was striking the keys on a pianoforte sharply when I arrived at the door of the Browns' flat. I tried to shake off the terrible sense of guilt I felt having just concocted an entire relationship between Agent Hunter and me for the benefit of Grand-mère Louvel's curiosity. If Agent Hunter ever got wind of the elaborate love affair between him and me that I'd just invented, I'd die of humiliation. But for now, the tale had done the job. The only problem that remained was she'd invited him to Christmas dinner and would not take no for an answer. But that was a problem for later.

"Again," a woman's voice called.

From inside, the soft voice of a young lady intoned:

God bless you merry, gentlemen,

Let nothing you dismay,

For Jesus Christ our Saviour
Was born on Christmas day.
To save poor souls from Satan's power,
When they had gone astray.
O tidings of comfort and joy

The singer had such a sweet voice, I hated to interrupt. Hearing a hesitation before the songbird restarted after striking the wrong note, I knocked on the door.

A moment later, a harried-looking woman answered. Her clothing was disheveled; her brown hair, which had been pulled back into a bun, had loose strands that flew all over the place. When she opened the door, she gave me a hard look, eyeing my bright red cape. Her eyes narrowed. Most people in London had at least heard rumor of the Red Cape Society. Whenever something unusual occurred in the city, we were not far behind. My red cape often made people eye me warily, as if by seeing me they were admitting to something they'd rather not acknowledge. In truth, most Londoners wouldn't want to know what was really creeping around in our city. But they suspected *something*. The look on the woman's face spoke volumes. It was that same mixed look of alarm, denial, and fear.

"Yes?" she said.

"Hello. Would it be possible for me to speak to Mister or Missus Brown?"

"I'm Missus Brown."

"Very good. I'm here about your son. I have just a few questions. Can I come in?"

Someone banged on the keys of the piano then footsteps retreated from the room.

"And you are?" she asked, eyeing the red cloak once more.

"Perhaps you will remember me. I'm Clemeny Louvel. I used to live near here. My superiors at the agency"—usually a vague enough description to get people to talk—"asked me to look into your son's disappearance."

"Clemeny Louvel? Madame Louvel's granddaughter?"

"Uh, yes. Since I'm from the area, the agency thought it would be best to send me."

Missus Brown nodded then stepped aside. "Please. Come in."

The little room was tidy and decorated for the upcoming holiday. Since Queen Victoria had started the fashion of decorating a spruce tree and keeping it in the house—a tradition I still didn't quite understand—many commoners had copied the fashion. A tree decorated with candles, gold and silver balls, and red bow, sat in one corner. The room smelled…woodsy. But it was also hot inside for which I was grateful. My fingers were still freezing.

"Have a seat, Miss Louvel," Missus Brown said. "I'll

be with you in a moment."

She retreated to the back of the house, where I heard her instructing someone to prepare tea. I eyed the room as I waited. A modest income afforded them some luxuries. The furniture was relatively new. The décor leaned toward the fashionable. As I eyed over the coatrack in the entryway, I spotted coats for a young lady, an adult female, and a young boy.

Missus Brown returned. "It's quite chilly outside. My daughter will prepare us some tea."

"Thank you. I know you have talked to the local authorities, but would you mind telling me about your son? When did he go missing? What happened?"

"It was a week ago. We had returned late in the afternoon. We'd gone to church, stopped by a friend's home for lunch, then made a stop at the grocer. When we returned, I asked the children to attend to their chores. My daughter, Arabella, was in the dining room setting the table for dinner. I was in the kitchen. Toby… well, he was in the room he shares with his sister. We heard a commotion in the back, and when we got there, the window was open and Toby was gone. Arabella crawled out the window, thinking Toby was playing on the rooftop again, but there was no one there. Someone took him through the window."

"And how old is your son?"

"Seven."

"Does he often play on the rooftop?"

Missus Brown shifted nervously. "He is a very spirited child. We have trouble keeping him from climbing on things."

Just then, a pretty girl entered. She carried a tray upon which sat two steaming cups of tea.

"Sugar?" she asked.

"No, thank you. Honey and lemon, perhaps?"

The girl nodded, her head full of blonde ringlets bouncing along with her. She set the tray down, added a slice of lemon and a dollop of honey to my cup, gave it a good stir, then handed the drink to me in the most mannerly of fashions.

"Thank you," I said.

She bobbed a little curtsey, served her mother, then sat down beside Missus Brown.

"Was anyone else at home at the time?" I asked then took a sip of tea. The blend was delicious, tart with flowery undertones, and perfectly brewed.

Missus Brown shook her head. "My husband had gone to visit a neighbor who was feeling ill. My husband is the apothecary, you see."

"Ahh," I said then nodded. "And your son…do you know what he was doing in the room? Napping? Reading?"

Missus Brown looked into her teacup. She took a deep breath then said, "He was sulking. I didn't permit him to eat cake before his dinner, so he'd worked himself up into a tantrum and then went off to sulk."

I smiled gently. "All children behave so at times. As do many adults."

It sounded to me like Tobias Brown was a bit of a handful. Of course, he was only a handful, not a hellion like Princess Helena, Her Majesty's youngest child. The princess's bad temper was the gossip of London. If one wanted to see a picture of devilry, there was no better place to look. But Tobias sounded simply like a spirited boy. No wonder his mother looked half-guilty. She'd probably wished someone would take the rambunctious boy off her hands for a moment.

"May I see the room?" I asked.

Missus Brown nodded then led me to the back, Arabella following discreetly behind us.

The little room had two neatly made beds, matching trunks at the end. Arabella's bed had a pretty doll sitting on it. On the other bed sat a wooden duck with wheels. Suspended from the ceiling was a model of the airship *Stargazer*. I smiled when I saw it. It was a good likeness. From what I could tell, nothing was out of place. The window faced the side of the building. The building next to it was lower. Someone could have climbed into the window, snagged the child, then went back out. Or, the child had climbed out, and something had happened.

Bracing myself for the cold, I opened the window. I slipped outside and onto the rooftop. I walked to the pinnacle of the neighboring roof and looked down the Strand. I scanned the rooftops. Some of the clay tiles on the roof were cracked as if something heavy had passed this way. A large man, perhaps? I frowned then looked over the side of the building. Too high to jump. Nothing to climb down. Whoever had taken the boy had carried him. But to where?

"The grounds all around were checked?" I called back to Missus Brown who was leaning out the window.

"Yes. The rooftops and the ground below. No sign of him."

I turned and stared across the city. How many nights had I chased the packs across these rooftops? I cast a glance toward Tinker's Tower which loomed large on the horizon. Even now someone was probably planning mayhem, and I was not there to keep them in check. Instead, I was chasing a kidnapping, a job better suited for a different branch of Her Majesty's law enforcement.

I crossed the rooftop then climbed back in through the window.

Once inside, I smoothed down my clothes. In my line of business, it didn't pay to go around wearing a dress. I was, in fact, wearing the same leather pants favored by female airship jockeys. My attire, it seemed, was not lost on Arabella, who stared at me in fascination.

I closed the window. "I have some other people to talk to. Is there anything else you noticed that day? Someone following you? Does your husband have any enemies, perhaps? Anything odd?"

Missus Brown shook her head. "No, no one. And my husband is beloved in this neighborhood."

"Very well then. If you don't mind, I'll show myself out."

Missus Brown nodded. "Of course. And thank you."

I headed back down the hallway. I needed to let Hunter know this was a dead-end. This assignment needed to be pitched back for another division to look into. This was not our beat.

"But Mother, shouldn't we tell her about the pear?"

Oh, hell's bells. Here we go.

I looked back at the girl who was standing in the hall. "Pear?"

"It's nothing, really," Missus Brown said.

I looked at the girl.

Arabella cleared her throat, took a deep breath to firm her resolve, then said, "After my brother was taken, we found a pear on his bed."

"A pear?"

She nodded. "Yes."

"Like the kind you eat?"

"Yes. It was yellow-colored. Golden, even. Like it had just been picked. It may be nothing. We'd been to the grocer earlier that day. Tobias may have lifted it without us seeing. He has a terrible habit of picking up things that do not belong to—"

"Arabella!"

"Well, it's true, Mother. If there is anyone who might understand that it's *unusual*, it's her," she said, glancing at the red cloak. "Maybe he picked it up from outside. I don't know. But still. It was strange."

I raised an eyebrow at her. "Indeed. That is noteworthy. Thank you for telling me."

Arabella cast a satisfied sidelong glance at her mother then bobbed a curtsey toward me.

"I'll call again soon," I said then headed back out.

A pear. A pear? Now, a pear might be a *nothing*—something little Tobias filched—or it could be a *something*. Odd indeed.

With that, I headed back outside and headed toward the grocer.

Time to go pear shopping.

CHAPTER 4
Saint Clement Danes

As I walked down the street, the bells on Saint Clement Danes let out their familiar chime. Though the nursery rhyme that had the lines, "oranges and lemons say the bells on Saint Clement's" referred to the other Saint Clement's church in the old City of London, Saint Clement Danes had also adopted a similar chime. Oranges and lemons, Grand-mère's favorite proclamation, filled the air.

Having left the grocer, who assured me he'd not had any pears this last month, I headed toward the Saint Clement Charity School and Orphanage from which two children had also gone missing.

I walked up the chapel steps, the feeling of dread filling my belly. Grand-mère Louvel had taken me in the moment she'd found me on the steps of the church that cold winter morning, and I'd spent my life attending

Saint Clement Danes. But walking up those steps, knowing my mother had left her infant child right there in a basket, always filled me with terrible loathing and sadness. I inhaled deeply then pushed my breath out. I needed to finish this case as soon as possible.

I pushed open the door to the church and entered. The domed ceiling was white and trimmed with gold fixtures, including the faces of cherubic angels. Light poured in from the tall domed windows. The pews were polished to a gleam and had been decorated with pine boughs and red velvet bows. The area around the altar had been similarly decorated for the holiday season. The place smelled of pine, old books, and aged upholstery. I cast a glance at the pipe organ on the balcony above the entrance. I had spent most of my youth sitting beside that organ, listening to Grand-mère play.

Pastor Rosenberry, who had been at the front of the church near the altar, looked up when I entered. His brow furrowed. He turned and walked to meet me.

"Miss Louvel," he said quietly so not to disturb an older woman and a gentleman who sat praying. "It's good to see you."

Civil as always. Fake civil, but civil. "You too, Pastor."

"What can I do for you? Is Madame Louvel well?" he asked. His eyes scanned my mangled face. Didn't he know it was rude to stare? Usually, such a gaze made me feel self-conscious, but with Pastor Rosenberry, I just felt annoyed.

"Oh yes, and in full form today. I am here, in fact, at the request of my agency. They have asked me to investigate the disappearances."

Father Rosenberry's eyebrows shot up so quickly that I thought they might fly off his brow. "*You*? They've sent *you* to investigate?"

I clenched my jaw. Pastor Rosenberry's belief that women should be gentle, meek, prayerful, and silent had never set well with my general nature. I recalled him being less than impressed when I'd joined the society. Seems he was still of the opinion that I might have better served the world bearing children and singing hymns. "Yes. *Me*," I said, hoping he didn't miss the sharpness of my retort.

He stiffened a bit—which seemed impossible—then said, "Very well. Come with me." He turned and headed toward the back.

As I passed down the center aisle, the gentleman who was praying looked up at me, his eyes dancing over my red cloak. His gaze met mine, and I saw deep sadness there. He nodded to me then turned back to his prayers.

Father Rosenberry led me to the back of the church and down the hallway to his office. Once I was inside, he closed the door behind me.

"I collated a file on each child. Both are orphans. Both went missing from their dorm room," he said, handing a folder to me.

"Any witnesses?"

"No. We've bolted up the window, and Pastor Clark has been sleeping there at night. No disturbances since Tom went missing."

"Any chance their absent parents came to retrieve them?"

"None. Lucas, the older boy, lost his parents to fever. And Tom, his junior henchman, came to us from a harlot."

"Henchman?"

"These two boys are thick as thieves and just as naughty. How many times have they been disciplined for fighting, stealing, cursing? At first, we thought they'd simply run off, joined up with some crew. But then other children in the neighborhood started disappearing, and all the other children in the orphanage swear the boys didn't have a plan to run away. The other children are frightened. That alone tells me something is wrong."

I nodded as I flipped through the papers. There were reports on both boys: their education, illnesses, and lists of their offenses, not limited to releasing a box of frogs during a sermon. I grinned as I read that one. Wicked little devils.

"May I talk to the other children?"

Pastor Rosenberry nodded. "They will be in their studies. Pastor Clark is with them now. Will anyone else from your agency be looking into the case? A superior, perhaps? This is a dire situation."

And one you, Clemeny, being a woman, cannot possibly handle.

"No. Her Majesty asked for me in particular for this case," I replied distractedly as if it were nothing.

"Her…Her Majesty?"

"Yes. There was a gentleman in the church praying. Who is he?"

Pastor Rosenberry cleared his throat twice, no doubt choking down his astonishment, then said, "That's Mister Anderson. His daughter is also missing."

"I don't remember him."

"His family moved to this area two years ago."

"I see. Are there any new congregation members of note? Or anything else you've noticed that seems…off?"

Pastor Rosenberry shook his head. "No. Not that I can think of."

"Very well. May I keep these awhile?" I asked, tapping the papers on the palm of my hand.

Pastor Rosenberry nodded.

"Thank you."

He gave me a curt nod then sat down at his desk. He

still had not shaken the bewildered expression from his face.

Smirking, I headed back into the church.

RM

Mister Anderson was at the front lighting a prayer candle. Wordlessly, I joined him. Lifting a taper, I lit a candle, always for my own mother, whomever she was, wherever she was, if she were still alive. One day, maybe, I would learn the truth about where I'd come from. But in the meantime, I needed Mister Anderson to talk.

"I-I'm sorry, miss, but I noticed your cloak," Mister Anderson said in a whisper.

"Shall we step outside?"

Mister Anderson nodded. He closed his eyes, said one inaudible prayer, made the sign of the cross, then turned and headed outside. I followed along behind him.

Saint Clement Danes sat on a small island between two sides of the following traffic on the Strand. A mix of buggies and coal or steam-powered vehicles rolled past. I frowned at the infernal machines and the racket they made, causing me to strain to hear as Mister Anderson asked, "Are you the one looking for our children?"

His question, however muted, was heartbreaking.

Tears clung to his lower lids. My regular beat never had me working with tearful fathers or rattled mothers. I suddenly wished I was chasing a wolf down some dark alley or flirting with Lionheart, which was a lot more fun. But even as I thought it, an image of Agent Hunter floated through my mind, popping the picture of Lionheart like a stray bubble.

"Yes," I said, trying to refocus. "Pastor Rosenberry said your daughter is missing?"

He nodded. "Elizabeth," he said, pressing a locket toward me. "She went missing three days back."

Another child not on the list. I took the golden locket from his hand and stared at the painted miniature of a lovely girl with black hair and light eyes. She was as pretty as a china doll. "What happened?" I asked.

"I put her down for bed, made a cup of tea, then went back to check on her. Her window was open. She was gone. I searched high and low for her. I couldn't find her anywhere," he said then burst into tears. "Who would take my child like that? Who would do something like that so close to Christmas?" he said with a rattling sob. "I put in a report to the Bow Street Runners. They said they would be by, but they haven't come yet."

"Where do you live, sir?"

"Down the Strand, near the Lyceum," he said, referring to the theatre.

"Please, write your address here," I said, pulling out a pad from my satchel and handing it along with a fountain pen to him. "And your wife, sir? She saw nothing?"

The man shook his head. "I am a widower. It's just my daughter and me."

"I'm very sorry. You said you put your daughter down to sleep. She disappeared at night?"

"Yes. I wouldn't have even known until morning except for the bird."

"I'm sorry, the bird?"

He nodded. "A colly bird got into the room through the open window. Somehow it got tangled up in a string on Elizabeth's blanket. It was squawking terribly. If it hadn't been for that racket, I wouldn't have known. As it was, I was too late. Please come by, Agent. Elizabeth is the last piece of her mother I have left. She's everything to me."

"I will. This evening. I promise."

He nodded.

I set a reassuring hand on his arm then turned to go.

A colly bird? Now, that *was* odd.

CHAPTER 5
Snips and Snails

"Boys. Boys, please take your seats," Pastor Clark was saying, sounding a bit exasperated, when I arrived at the classroom door. The orphanage and charity school sat just across the street from the church. It was a large, two-story structure. On the first floor was the schoolroom, kitchen, a small parlor, and an office. The upper floor had two rooms for the children—one dormitory for the boys and one for the girls—and housing for Pastor Clark and Pastor Rosenberry. Missus Miller, who lived down the street, also worked at the school. She watched the girls and prepared the meals. She let me in and directed me to the classroom.

I stood just outside the open classroom door and watched Pastor Clark. For many months, Grand-mère was very sure I should let Pastor Clark woo me, much to my horror. I didn't mind that he was plump—I imagined that a stout man would be a fine thing to have in bed on a cold winter's night—and godly, but he perpetually smelled of sardines and always stood too close, like he wanted to shove his tongue down my throat the minute he got the chance. Once or twice, I'd thought about stabbing him.

I leaned against the doorframe and looked inside. The girls were sitting, waiting attentively. The boys, however, had broken out into a squabble.

"Boys! Take your seats," Pastor Clark called once more.

I cleared my throat loudly.

At the sound of a newcomer, the boys dispensed with their squabble and sat. All the children turned to stare at me.

"Miss Louvel," Pastor Clark exclaimed, seemingly taken aback by my presence. He turned to join me then stumbled over the leg on his podium and tripped.

I stepped forward to catch him in the sincerest hope that I wouldn't have to. I thanked God that Pastor Clark was able to right himself in time.

The class chuckled.

"Oh! Oh my," he exclaimed, smoothing down his suit and patting down his pin-straight bowl-cut hair as he regained his footing. His cheeks burned red. As I looked around the room, I noticed all the boys' hair was cut in a similar fashion. They looked like a miniature Norman invasion. I'd have to have a word with Grand-mère, see if she could make a not-so-subtle suggestion for a proper barber for the boys. "Miss Louvel, whatever are you doing here?"

"The agency sent me about the missing boys."

The smiles around the room faded.

"Oh," Pastor Clark said in surprise. His expression, however, lacked the disdain I'd seen on Pastor Rosenberry's face. "Shall we go downstairs to the office? Children, take out your readers and—"

"No. No," I said with a wave of the hand. "I'd like to talk to the children."

"Oh. Yes. Of course," he said then pulled out a chair for me, setting it in front of the class.

I smiled at him. Sardine smell aside, Pastor Clark really was a nice chap. I could see why Grand-mère suggested him. But he lacked a certain edge—and well-groomed mutton chops—that I needed in a man. I took a seat.

"Hello, children. I'm Clemeny. Missus Louvel is my grandmother. Do you all know her?"

They nodded, relaxing a bit.

"I understand Lucas and Tom are missing. I'm here to find out what happened. Can any of you tell me what happened the day Lucas disappeared?"

"It was night, ma'am," a little boy said.

"Sorry?"

"He didn't disappear in the day. He disappeared at night."

"Is that right?" I asked, turning to Pastor Clark who nodded.

"And Tom? Did he disappear at night too?" I asked.

The children nodded.

"Tom went missing from our room," one of the boys said.

"And Lucas? From the room as well?" I asked.

The children wouldn't make eye contact with me.

I turned to Pastor Clark who looked confused.

"Children? Yes, Lucas went missing from his room. He wasn't in his bed in the morning."

I turned back to the children. The girls looked just as confused as Pastor Clark. The boys, however, were shifting nervously. One boy was looking everywhere but at me. "You there," I said, pointing to him. "What's your name?"

The boy froze then turned to me, his eyes wide. "W-William."

"Did Lucas go missing from the room?"

I hadn't thought it possible, but the child's eyes grew even larger.

"The truth, now," I said, pushing aside my cloak to reveal the handle of the pistol on my side.

"Miss Louvel," Pastor Clark whispered.

Smirking, I gave Pastor Clark a knowing half-wink—a move I had yet to perfect with my right eye—then wished I hadn't when I saw his cheeks redden.

"No. No, ma'am. He didn't," William said.

"Then where was he?" I asked.

"There's a girl. She lives with some of the other kids down by the river. He went to see her but never came back."

Pastor Clark gasped. "Children! Why didn't you tell us?"

"Because Pastor Rosenberry told Lucas not to see that guttersnipe anymore, and *you* said if Lucas got in trouble one more time, Pastor Rosenberry was going to send him away," William exclaimed.

Pastor Clark huffed. "You should have told us. I'm very sorry, Miss Louvel. I didn't know."

"Not to worry. William, is it possible Lucas is still with the other children? Maybe he decided not to come back."

William shook his head. "No. Bunny came crying looking for him the next day. I-I think she saw something."

"Bunny?"

"His girl."

"Did any of you see anything, maybe the night Tom went missing?"

"I smelled peppermint," said a little boy, perhaps no older than five.

The others giggled.

I smiled at the child. He was a sweet little thing with blond hair and wide blue eyes, and he was missing his two front teeth. "What's your name?" I asked him.

"Edward."

"Edward, you smelled peppermint the night Tom went missing?"

"Don't listen to Edward, ma'am. He likes to make up stories," one of the older boys said.

"I do not!" the little boy protested. "I did smell peppermint, really strong like someone had opened up a tin of candies. But there was a bad feeling in the room, so I hid under my covers and closed my eyes. Tom was gone the next day. My bed is right beside Tom's."

"Thank you, Edward. Anyone else notice something amiss?

"I-I heard something," a quiet voice called from the back.

The class turned to a small boy who wore spectacles.

"You did?" Pastor Clark said in surprise. "Charles, what did you hear?"

Everyone looked at the boy.

"Something big and loud on the roof. Footsteps and bells."

Pastor Clark leaned toward me. "That's more than this boy said all week."

"Very good. Thank you, Charles."

He smiled shyly then sunk down lower in his seat.

"You will you find them, ma'am, won't you?" William asked.

"I promise to do my best."

"Like we even want Tom back," one of the boys grumbled.

I looked around the crowd to see a little boy with a very black eye.

"And whose handiwork is that?" I asked the boy, pointing to his eye.

"Tom's," he groused.

"Yes, well, Tom is a spirited boy, but we're making progress. With the Lord's help, he will turn it around," Pastor Clark assured me.

"Quite the shiner, but you'll recover in no time. Take it from me," I told the boy, tapping my eyepatch.

The buy huffed a laugh.

I turned to the girls. "Did you any of you hear or see anything?"

They all shook their heads.

"And none of the girls are missing?" I asked Pastor Clark.

"No. Missus Miller has taken to sleeping in the girl's

dorm at night to ensure their safety. And I am staying with the boys."

"And no other disturbances or odd noises? Anything else? Anything peculiar?"

They all shook their heads.

"There were the hens, though," said one little girl with dark hair. "The morning after Tom disappeared, we found three hens in the garden. They appeared out of nowhere."

"And they were delicious," Pastor Clark said, rubbing his round stomach.

The children laughed with him.

"A gift, we think, from a parishioner," Pastor Clark reassured me.

"Which parishioner?"

"Oh. Well, we aren't sure."

I nodded.

"The girl Lucas was courting. You said her name is Bunny? Where can I find her?" I asked, turning back to William.

The others looked at him.

He shrugged. "Their crew works the Strand. At night, they have a place near Waterloo Bridge," he said, his eyes darting from Pastor Clark, who was frowning hard at him, to me.

"Thank you. Mind if I have a look around before I go?" I asked Pastor Clark then rose before he could protest. "Study hard, children. Christmas is coming. Surely Pastor Clark has something special planned for you. Perhaps some plum pudding?"

The children looked at Pastor Clark expectantly.

He smiled. "Maybe. Maybe. God rewards the hardworking, the virtuous. So, let's get to it once more. Take out your readers."

With a nod to Pastor Clark, I exited quickly before it occurred to him to chaperone me around the building. I headed upstairs to the boys' dormitory. There were twelve small beds, all neatly made, but the room was very stark. I went to the single window and looked out across the rooftops, keeping in mind what Charles said. He'd definitely heard something on the rooftop, and Edward had smelled peppermint. That one still had me puzzled. I climbed out the window onto the roof of the next building. Then, grabbing the ledge, I hoisted myself up on top of the roof of the charity school. The peak of the school had a good view of the Strand. I could see the roofs of the buildings at King's College. Would Lionheart be there now?

A cold wind whipped, blowing my cape around me and stirring up a light whirlwind of snow. I scanned the neighborhood. If the first abduction had happened at the Brown household, the second at the Orphanage, the third near Waterloo Bridge, then down to Mister Anderson's address near the Lyceum, someone was working the Strand. And whoever was doing the lifting, they were doing it after the sun went down. That sounded very werewolf-like.

Templar Pack ruled this part of town. Had one of his pack members gone astray? As quickly as the thought occurred to me, I dismissed it. The image of the Templars in their glittering armor outside the airship hangar the night we'd taken out Cyril flashed through my mind. The Templars were loyal. None of them had gone astray in hundreds of years.

Rogue dog, maybe? Someone trying to encroach on Lionheart's territory just to piss off the new alpha?

I wasn't sure.

I briefly thought about stopping by King's College and checking in with Lionheart, but my thoughts went to Bryony Paxton. I liked Professor Paxton. I honestly did. But no matter how much I liked her, it didn't curb the jealousy I felt. I had no business getting involved with Lionheart, but I liked his attention. It made me feel special. The fact that he had found someone to love—someone who wasn't me—made me hurt in a way I didn't understand. I hadn't found a way to squelch the feeling. Better to leave well enough alone.

No, I wouldn't bother Lionheart with this. Whoever was nabbing the children, they would have to tangle with me.

CHAPTER 6
What the Dickens?

I headed down the Strand toward Waterloo Bridge. I was about turn down Arundel Street when I noticed a bit of commotion ahead. The Bow Street Boys appeared to be talking—well, half-talking, half-roughing up—a group of kids. I approached the group, listening to the conversation as I drew near.

I blew on my fingers once more. I didn't remember it being this cold at Christmas last year, and it had already snowed much more than usual in London. I pulled a silver flask from my belt, took a quick sip of brandy to warm me, and then approached the crowd.

"Honest, Officer. We found 'em," a boy was saying.

"He's telling the truth, mister. Maybe the river washed 'em up," a second lad added.

"Yeah, maybe the Thames washed 'em up," a small girl chirped in.

"You know what the punishment is for stealing," one of the officers was saying as he grabbed the biggest boy by the collar on his shirt.

The second officer grabbed the other two children by the arms and was about to haul them off to the paddy wagon parked nearby.

"Officers? Problem?" I asked.

"Not to worry, ma'am. We've got it settled," one of the officers called without looking up.

The children looked from the officers to me.

I pulled up my hood and adjusted my cape so it draped about me in an obvious fashion. "That wasn't what I asked, Officer," I retorted.

Exasperation filled the man's voice. "Look, lady," he began as he turned to me. But when his eyes took in the cape, he let the boy go.

Pushing my cape aside to reveal the small emblem of the Red Cape Society on my belt, I raised a questioning eyebrow at the man.

The officer nudged his partner, who frowned then looked over his shoulder. When he spotted me, he let go of the children he was holding.

The kids, thinking it was their cue to run like hell, moved to take off. But I raised a finger, motioning to them, and they stilled like statues.

"Let me ask once more. What is the issue here?" I said.

"Um, well, nothing for you to be worried about, Agent. Just some pickpockets trying to fence their stolen goods."

"We didn't steal anything," the older boy protested.

"And what is it that you didn't steal?" I asked the boy, looking from him to the officers and back again.

"These," the other officer said, extending his hand. Therein lay five perfect golden bands.

"Rings?"

Both officers and the children nodded.

I looked at the children. "Where did you find them?"

"By the river," the girl said.

"Where? On a road? A walking path? Near the shore?"

"They were lying in the mud not far from our camp by the bridge," one the boys answered.

"You see, they're lying," one of the officers told me.

"Has anyone reported missing jewelry to your station?" I asked the officer.

"Well, no. But—"

"But they have reported missing children, haven't they? Isn't your station supposed to be looking into that matter, not bothering a bunch of street rats?"

"Yeah, well, we were working on that case when these kids caused a ruckus."

"Ruckus? We 'bout had these sold until you showed up," the shorter boy protested. "No ruckus about it."

I pulled out my journal, jotted down Mister Anderson's address, then tore out the page. "Mister Anderson, the gentleman who lives at this address, has been waiting on your department to call. His daughter is missing. I am sure your superiors are aware that my *division* is now on the case. I expect you to follow up on this lead immediately," I said, handing the paper to the second officer while scooping the rings from his other hand. "And I'll take care of these."

"We-we didn't know that the Society was working the case," the first officer said.

"You do now. So scuttle off and do your job."

"Yes, Miss—"

"Agent. Agent Louvel."

"Sorry. Yes, Agent," the officer said, then he and his comrade crawled back onto their wagon and headed off in the direction of Mister Anderson's home.

I looked at the rings. They were identical, each made of high-quality gold. My brow furrowed as I thought it over.

"You said more children went missing?" the young girl asked.

Shaken from my thoughts, I looked up at her. "Yes. In fact, I was coming to find you to ask about another missing child."

"Bunny, Mags, Little Max, or Big Max?" the older boy asked.

"Sorry? What? I was looking for Bunny. I believe she might know something about the disappearance of a boy from Saint Clement Danes. Lucas?"

"Lucas is missing too?" the younger boy asked.

I stared at them. "Are you saying Bunny is missing?"

The three children nodded.

"And Mags, Big Max, and Little Max," the older boy added.

"What? Four children? Did you tell the authorities?"

They laughed.

"You see how well they believe us," the older boy said.

I sighed. He was right about that.

"When did these other children go missing?"

"Let's see…Mags, Little Max, and Big Max went missing last week. Bunny went missing last night. We didn't want to say in front of the Bow Street clods, but we found these rings right near her cot at our spot down by the river."

"That's very odd."

"We're a bit scared, to be honest. Someone is snatching us off the street."

"How many are you?"

"Us three and two more back at the bridge."

"I want you all to go to Saint Clement Danes. Ask for Pastor Clark. Tell him Agent Louvel insists that you all be given shelter until this case is settled."

"But didn't they snag Lucas and Tom from Saint Clement?"

"Tom, yes. But it appears Lucas was grabbed somewhere between courting Miss Bunny and the orphanage."

"All the same to you, miss. We're better off on the street."

"Clearly not. Four of you are missing! You will be safe at the orphanage. I…I believe the danger has passed there now, but not out here. You are still at risk if you are on the street at night." If my initial estimate was right, whomever was working the Strand would not backtrack to pick up these children but would move on…but where and why?

"You sure?"

"Positive."

"I'm not staying though. We'll go for a few days. Maybe through Christmas. That would be a good racket, something warm to eat on Christmas morning. What do you say?" the older boy said.

The others looked more hesitant.

"Tell Pastor Clark that I will sponsor your stay, if needed. But I want you off the streets. Today."

"But we aren't staying for good," the little girl confirmed.

"No. Of course not. Just until the trouble has passed. And I do believe the orphanage provides a nice

Christmas dinner. You must promise me you will go. I don't want to ask the other officers in my agency to remove you," I said, darkening my tone a bit.

Once more, I saw that same awe—and a little fear—that my cloak always evoked.

"Yes, ma'am," the older boy said with a nod.

"The others—Mags, Little Max and Big Max—where did they disappear?"

The older boy shrugged. "They were working the streets that night. You know, theatre crowd. Fancy dresses. Deep pockets. Lots of autos and carriages. Good hunting grounds. Everyone is out for the big holiday shows and the Lyceum and Adelphi."

I smirked but said nothing. Ripe for pickpocketing and panhandling. Of course. "And your camp. It's by the bridge?"

They nodded.

"Good. Now, go to Saint Clement. Understood?"

They nodded then turned and set off in a run. I only hoped they did what they were told. If I was right, they would be safe at the orphanage. But they were not safe on the street. That was certain. The case was out of hand. Nine children were missing. Nine, not four. Whatever was hunting the Strand, I needed to catch it and fast.

CHAPTER 7

The Nutcracker

After a quick investigation of the guttersnipe's camp, finding nothing odd save a bevy of swans swimming in the chilly Thames, I headed back toward the Strand. It was almost dusk when I arrived at Mister Anderson's flat on Burleigh Street. The apartment was in a finely appointed building; Mister Anderson's lodgings were on an upper floor. A footman met me at the door and led me into the parlor that was festively decorated with evergreens and a Christmas tree. I stood, my hands behind my back, and looked out the window down the street toward the Lyceum. A flurry of activity was underway as the theatre hands prepared for that night's show. From the window, I could see a sign advertising the event: *The Red Slipper Ballet Academy presents The Nutcracker.*

"Miss—Agent Louvel," Mister Anderson called, entering behind me. "Please, have a seat."

"I was just admiring the view," I said then sat.

"Ah, yes. The theatre. My daughter and I love the shows. We never miss one. We'd been hoping to see *The Nutcracker*. They say the ballerina playing Clara is the best dancer since Elyse Murray graced the stage. Perhaps…perhaps there will still be time. Tea? Or brandy, perhaps?"

Given how cold it was outside and the fact that I was likely going to be up all night, I went for the brandy. Mister Anderson poured me a glass then handed me a snifter full of the amber-colored liquid. He then poured one for himself and took a seat opposite mine.

"I must thank you. The constables were by not long ago and took a full report."

I smirked. *Of course they were.* "I'm sorry it took them so long. Now, what can you tell me about your daughter's disappearance?"

"I am a manager at the bank," he said, pointing down the street. "I'd come home late, but Elizabeth's nanny was here with her all day. She didn't report anything unusual. Elizabeth and I had dinner, read a bit, then I tucked her in for bed. It was sometime around midnight when I heard the bird, as I mentioned to you earlier."

"Yes. The colly bird. And your nanny? Did she see anything unusual? Any disturbances during the day?"

The man shook his head then took a drink. "No. Nothing. Agent Louvel, Elizabeth is my princess, my everything. Everyone told me to send her to a boarding school, someplace proper for a young lady, but I couldn't let her go. If I had, this might never have happened. We…we need to find her."

"Mister Anderson, do you—and forgive me for asking—do you have any enemies? Anyone who might hold ill will against you?"

"I don't think so. Small grievances, perhaps. Loans I have declined. A certain lady whose intentions I rebuked. Nothing so serious to warrant something like this."

"May I see Elizabeth's room?"

He nodded then motioned for me to follow him. The small flat had beautiful, new furniture and lovely paintings on the walls. Mister Anderson was not a gentleman but certainly a man of some means. When he opened the door to young Elizabeth's room, however, one might have thought themselves at Buckingham Palace. I was unable to suppress a gasp.

Mister Anderson chuckled. "Even Princess Helena would be jealous, I suppose. I do spoil my Elizabeth a bit."

A bit was an understatement. The room looked like it

had vomited pink lace, silk, dresses, dolls, hats, and every other manner of thing a young lady could want. Most of Mister Anderson's wages must have gone to keeping his daughter in the latest fashion.

"The window, there, was open," Mister Anderson said. I went to the window and looked out. Unlike the other windows, this one did not lead to another rooftop. There was, however, a sturdy ledge that ran along the side of the building. The leap from there was not impossible. Difficult, but not impossible. Especially if you are a werewolf.

I turned back and looked at the room once more. Miss Elizabeth had to be the most spoiled child in all of England. I wondered if Her Majesty's children had so many beautiful dolls and gowns.

"I will need the name and address for your nanny and any other household staff," I told Mister Anderson, who had become teary-eyed once more. I handed him my notepad.

"Of course," he said, jotting down the names. "I…I don't know how I can live with myself if she's… harmed. My last words to her were harsh."

"Why so?"

"Elizabeth is my princess. And some of her demands are a bit excessive. With the holidays at hand, her desire for extravagances was beginning to outweigh what this Santa Claus could afford. And she was not pleased when I asked her to scale back for the sake of Santa Claus's reindeer."

"All children dream big," I said.

"Do they?" Mister Anderson replied. "In my effort to give her everything I didn't have, to make up for her loss of her mother, I fear I have overdone what was needed." He sighed then handed the notepad back to me.

I slid the journal back into my bag. "You only did your best. It's clear you love your daughter very much. I will do everything I can to find her and will send word as soon as I have news."

Mister Anderson nodded then led me back to the front of the flat. "Thank you, Agent Louvel."

With a nod, I headed back outside. The sun had set. It was time to find some high ground. When I exited the building, however, I caught the scents of roasted walnuts and crepes on the breeze. My stomach growled. A little detour wouldn't hurt, right? I followed my nose back out the Strand where the theatres were lit up. A line had already formed outside the Lyceum for the evening performance of *The Nutcracker*. I eyed the crowd. An elderly woman with startling white hair, wearing a shimmering white gown and bright red silk slippers, exited an auto that had just pulled up outside. The assembled crowd stopped to stare, clapping loudly when the woman emerged. She was accompanied by a distinguished-looking gentleman in a grey suit with a blue rose on the lapel. The woman waved to the crowd as she headed into the theatre. She must have been a famous actress, but I didn't follow the fine arts. I did, however, follow my nose. The street vendor had to be around here somewhere.

I headed away from the Lyceum and down toward the Adelphi. The marquee noted that they would be performing Charles Dickens' *A Christmas Carol*. A play about ghosts? Now, that was something I could enjoy. Better than the play, however, was the cart outside selling mulled wine.

"One, please," I told the man.

He looked at my cape then handed the drink to me. When I tried to press my coins toward him, he waved them away. "On me," he said with a wink.

Sipping the hot wine, cinnamon, orange, and other spices heavy on my tongue, my thoughts drifted toward Agent Hunter once more. My mind twisted past the lusty thoughts of his spicy skin to the soft smile on his face, and his kind words of caution as I'd headed out that morning. In truth, I knew almost nothing about him. What manner of man was he? Did he like the theatre or did he prefer the pub? Did he spend the weekends in the city, out in the country on a hunt, or curled up by a fire reading books? A firm derriere and bulging biceps aside, these were the things that made up who the man really was. And despite my most ardent fantasies about him, I really didn't know him at all. Sadly.

I trailed down the street, stopping to purchase a crepe with hazelnut and cocoa spread, then headed down an alleyway. Polishing off the last of my wine and gobbling down the crepe with such lack of decorum that Grand-mère would have been scandalized, I grabbed a ladder and climbed up to the rooftop. From there, it would merely be a matter of leapfrogging from rooftop to rooftop until I found a good spot. I eyed the sky. A week until the full moon. Some of the wolves, especially the older ones, would already be drawn out by the moonlight.

I found a spot beside a chimney, absorbing the heat off the bricks. I cast a glance across the snow-covered rooftops. The glow of the waxing moon cast a blue-silver sheen over everything, making the powder sparkle. I could hear the soft sounds of the orchestra in the theater below and the muted hum of voices, autos, and clopping horse hooves. But otherwise, it was silent.

"Well, Fenton, looks like it's just you and me," I said with a sigh, patting the hide hanging from my belt.

I stared out at the vista of gables. Trouble or no, I would find the werewolf running rampant on the Strand and end him.

CHAPTER 8
Up on the Rooftop

I stayed on the rooftop long after the theatre revelers had departed. Snatches of laughter and peals of "Away in a Manger" reached my ears. In the sky above, airships boasting red and green lanterns passed by. Christmas had come once more.

The clock on Tinker's Tower had just bonged out two in the morning when a light snow started to fall. I hadn't slept for more than twenty hours. I was freezing, my fingers and nose numb. My crepe long gone, my stomach started grumbling once more.

I was beginning to worry I had miscalculated. Perhaps the culprit was already working further down the Strand. I suddenly wished I'd ordered more uniformed officers on the streets. I hadn't done so since all they generally did was get in the way. But just as I started second guessing myself, the palms of my hands and bottom of my feet tingled.

A block away, a flock of birds was startled from their roost and flew off.

I slipped on my night optic and activated it. Wrapping one hand around my silver dagger and pulling my pistol from my belt, I stayed close to the chimney to hide in the shadowed darkness then scanned the nearby rooftops.

Save for the few airships passing overhead, almost nothing else was moving. The lamplights on the streets below flickered, casting orange blobs of light onto the silent streets. Both the rooftops and the road were covered with a light dust of snow that shimmered crystalline in the darkness.

Through this silent space, I heard bells. Jingle bells. Just like Charles had said.

I squeezed the handle on my knife and looked around. There, five buildings down the Strand, a shape appeared on the rooftop. From his massive size and the heavy robes he was wearing, he appeared to be a werewolf. But I didn't recognize him, and he was wearing some kind of strange hat. Wonderful. Just what I needed, another wild card like Marlowe. The hulking figure moved quickly across the rooftops.

Slinking from chimney to chimney to stay out of sight, I turned and headed in the direction of the figure who now lurked outside the window of a nearby building. He stood on a ledge, looking down into the window from the adjoining building's roof. I was too far away to see what he was hunting, but it didn't matter. I knew his quarry. What I didn't know was why the wolf was stalking children. Except, of course, for the most apparent reason. Children were tasty treats. Yet still, it had been years since we'd had that kind of problem, and never from the Templars. Such animalism was far beneath them.

Moving in quickly and quietly, I watched him work. His odd robe hung in tatters around his ankles. He also wore something on his back. A bag? A basket? That must be where he stuffed the children so he could make a hasty escape. I moved closer, darting from chimney to chimney, until I could get a clear line of fire. Most wolves backed off when they saw the red cape. Most, but not all.

Though it was very dim, only the light of the moon showing the wolf in shadow, I saw that he was moving into place. He reached out for the window frame.

I stepped out from behind the chimney, training my pistol, which was loaded with silver bullets, on him.

"Step back. Now," I said stiffly.

The figure froze in place.

"By proclamation of Her Majesty and under articles of the Red Cape Society, you are under arrest. I strongly suggest you don't move. I do have a license to shoot you on sight. Now, step back and turn around. Slowly."

The figure treaded back.

I squeezed my hand on the pistol tighter, my finger on the trigger. This was going to go one of two ways. And any second now, I'd know which.

"On your knees, wolf."

To my surprise, the figure started to chuckle. A wind blew across the rooftop, sweeping past the werewolf to me. I expected—and was used to—the sharp feral scent of werewolves. Instead, I smelled peppermint.

My heart beat harder.

"I said, on your knees."

Again, he laughed. Then he turned to face me, stepping more fully into the light of the moon.

Cat-like yellow eyes stared out from a grotesque face. A forked tongue slipped out from between fat lips. He laughed once more, snarling at me. The odd hat he'd been wearing wasn't a hat at all but horns and a thick mat of hair. He wore a ragged green robe trimmed with bells. Sneering, he moved toward me, stomping across the roof tiles with cloven feet.

"Demon," I whispered.

The creature laughed again, then turned and took off in a run, the bells on his clothes jingling.

Bracing myself, I took aim and fired.

The sound of my gunshot echoed across the city. The creature flinched but kept running.

Hell's bells. Move, Clemeny.

I sprinted behind him. The creature ran, leaping from rooftop to rooftop as it retreated down the Strand. My heart thundered as I raced to keep up with him. Dodging patches of ice and doing my best not to slip on the snow-covered rooftops, I followed the massive creature as he ran. But even if I caught him, then what? I knew very little about fighting demons. I wasn't equipped for the job in the slightest.

As I ran, I saw drops of blood on the rooftops. At least I had winged him. Shooting was something I did know how to do. I raced after him. His speed was incredible. Not just incredible, supernatural. And I was quickly running out of rooftops as Trafalgar Square appeared in the distance.

Just as I realized I needed to find a way down before he did, the creature stopped at the edge of a building and looked back at me. His yellow eyes glowed in the darkness. I saw that long, snake-like tongue slip from between his sharp teeth once more, then he turned and jumped.

Double hell's bells!

Racing to the ledge, I grabbed the ladder and climbed down. I ran to the other side of the building, but the creature was nowhere in sight. On the ground, however, I spotted blood then made out hoofprints larger than the palm of my hand.

From Trafalgar Square, I heard a horse whinny loudly, followed by the sound of men shouting.

I raced in that direction.

Two men who had a cart parked by the massive Christmas tree that decorated the square were trying to calm the wide-eyed horse.

"Did you see it? Which way did it go?"

"What? See who?"

"That…man."

"I didn't see anything. We were sleeping. Someone spooked the horse," the man said in a grumpy huff as he tried to calm his steed once more.

Dammit.

Scanning the ground, I spotted another drop of blood. I then spotted hoofprints in the snow. They were headed in the direction of the Mall. I raced behind the creature, trying to track hoofprints and drops of blood as I went. Soon, however, I had followed the hoofprints away from the promenade and into Saint James Park. Under the cover of the trees, I lost the trail. It was too dark. I stopped and listened. No jingle bells. I closed my eyes and inhaled deeply. No peppermint. I tried to feel for the creature. Nothing. Opening my eyes once more, I yanked off my optic and looked with my mooneye. I stood among the leafless trees, their shadowy silhouettes making long claws on the ground. I looked toward Buckingham Palace. The lights from the palace windows seemed to bob amongst the trees. There was a demon here, this close to the royal residence. A demon. Right here. I waited in the darkness, looking and listening. There was nothing. The creature was gone.

A short while later, I heard someone approach.

"Oi," a voice called. "Hold it right there now. What are you doing out here?"

I looked back to see one of the guards who patrolled the Mall walking toward me.

I slipped my gun back into my belt and grabbed my small silver badge.

Frowning toward the dark woods where the beast had disappeared, I turned toward the guardsman.

"I said, what are you—"

"Yeah, yeah. I heard you," I said, lifting my badge. "Got an auto nearby?"

"What? Oh, I see. Sorry, Agent. Auto? No. I have a horse. What's going on here?"

"I need your horse. And you need to get extra men patrolling this area. I chased…a…well, a vagrant, into the park but lost him in the darkness."

"Yeah, we chase thieves out of here all the time. They use the park for cover just to—"

"No. Listen to me. You need extra men on the Mall. Do you understand me? Tell them Agent Louvel of the

Red Cape Society has requested increased security. And if anything—*anything*—is found out of order, you need to inform my superiors at once. Now, where is your horse?"

"My horse? There," the guard said, looking back toward the promenade.

I looked around him, catching sight of the horse in the moonlight. "I'll bring him back when I can," I said then passed the guard who stood staring at me. "Hop to it, man. There is a menace in these woods."

"What…what do I tell the others we're on the lookout for?" the guard called.

A demon. "A kidnapper. Disguised as a satyr."

"Are you…Are you serious?"

"Do I look like I'm joking? I have on the red cape. You should expect the weird. Get to work, solider," I said. Finding the guard's steed, I mounted the horse and headed away from the park. I knew almost nothing about hunting demons. Luckily, there was one person in our agency who was renowned for the task. And it was the one person I was happiest to have an excuse to visit. Agent Hunter.

CHAPTER 9
Meanwhile, in Covent Garden

I rode the guard's horse to Covent Garden where Agent Hunter lived. The townhouse—not a flat—was located in a block that had once been very fashionable before Londoners had decided Mayfair was the better choice for those of wealth and distinction. Either Agent Hunter was making a far better salary than he let on or had acquired some wealth due to inheritance. Both points were of interest to me. But then, everything about Agent Hunter was of interest to me. Which was how I knew where he lived. Apparently, he'd hosted a gathering when he first took over from Agent Greystock, but I'd still been in Nottingham recovering and had missed it, a point I always regretted after getting a look at him. Now I had a good reason to stop by.

The first light of dawn burned off the darkness and

turned the sky a hazy yellowish-gray color. It was freezing, and I was exhausted. I tied the horse to a pole outside, went to the townhouse door, and rang.

And then I waited.

A lamplighter was working his way down the street toward me, singing a carol as he went. I stood rubbing my hands together as he hummed the last lines of "God Rest Ye Merry Gentlemen."

"Early morning, miss?" he called, stopping to extinguish the lamp nearest Agent Hunter's house.

"Late night, actually."

He chuckled. "Good weather for a hot toddy."

"Or three."

"Or four!"

We laughed.

There was a click as the door opened.

"Yes?"

I looked back to see a bedraggled butler at the door. "My apologies. Good morning. It is imperative that I speak to Agent Hunter."

The man cleared his throat, slid his spectacles down his nose, and studied me.

"Please tell him Agent Louvel is here."

"Very well," the man said then closed the door behind him.

Rubbing my hands together, I turned to watch the

lamplighter work his way down the street. He whistled a merry tune, another Christmas carol, as he walked. At first, I paid little attention to it, thinking only of a hot toddy and a warm bath. My mind tripped over the idea that Agent Hunter likely had a large, claw-footed tub somewhere in his stylish townhouse, and that it could, no doubt, fit two. I was about to plunge into the fantasy when the lamplighter's song—he'd switched to actually singing the lyrics rather than whistling—caught my attention.

"Five golden rings. Four colly birds, three French hens, two turtle doves, and a partridge in a pear tree," he sang then started the song over once more, rounding back to the sixth day of Christmas.

Five *golden rings.*

Four *colly birds.*

Three French *hens.*

Two turtle doves?

And a partridge in a *pear* tree.

"Agent Louvel?" a voice called from the door behind me.

I turned and looked back to find Agent Hunter standing there in fitness clothing, his hands taped in the manner of a boxer, sweat dripping from his brow.

"I…Agent Hunter…good. I need your help," I said as I stepped past him and into the foyer of his home, counting on my fingers as I went.

"Help? With what? It's not even dawn. Is that…is that a palace guard horse?"

"Uh, yes. I borrowed him from a guard at the Mall. Listen, it's not a wolf abducting the children," I said then leaned in closer to Agent Hunter so his butler couldn't hear. "It's a demon. I saw him—and shot him—last night. But I lost his trail in the Mall. He was about to abduct another child when I chased him down."

"A demon? Are you certain?" Agent Hunter asked, closing the door behind me as he began to peel the tape off his hands.

"Very."

Agent Hunter nodded. "Martin, please escort Agent Louvel to the library. I…" he said then looked down at his attire. "I'll change and join you in a moment. I was exercising."

I could not prevent myself from following his gaze down across his open-necked blousy shirt to his pugilist's pants, skintight fitness trousers favored by bare-knuckled boxers. They were far too tight and very revealing. To my shock, I felt a blush rise to my cheeks. I looked away.

"Um. O-okay," I said stupidly. *Well done, Clemeny.*

Agent Hunter coughed abashedly. "Martin, please ask Marianna to prepare breakfast for Agent Louvel."

"Very well, sir. This way, Agent," the butler said then motioned for me to follow him.

The man led me to the library toward the back of the townhouse. The walls were lined from floor to ceiling with books. A tall window looked out on the small, enclosed conservatory in the back of the house. Despite the fact that a scattering of snowflakes fell on the windowpanes above the greenhouse, leafy green plants and flowers grew in the small space. A fire was already burning in the hearth. I went beside it and warmed myself. I eyed the room with great curiosity. A long table in the middle of the library was stacked with books and scattered with notes. I could see that Agent Hunter had been researching lore. He had a map of Carfax Sanatorium laid out as well as a yellowed map of the ancient ruins of Roman Londinium.

I scanned the room. A chair had been pulled close to the fireplace. A small stack of books, a pipe, and a tin of tobacco sat on the table beside it. But no lady's portrait kept Agent Hunter company. And there was only one chair by the fire, not two. Good.

The door opened once more, and Agent Hunter reappeared. He wore a pair of simple gray wool trousers, a waistcoat, and a clean shirt. It was apparent he'd dressed with some urgency. He was still unshaven.

"I am sorry to intrude like this," I said. *Liar.* "But I need your help."

"Of course," he said then motioned for me to come sit at the table. "You said you shot it?"

"Yes."

"With what?"

"Silver bullet."

Agent Hunter nodded. "Silver, of course, can harm a demon but not kill it. No gun can. The only way to rid ourselves of a demon is to determine what manner of creature he is and then vanquish him."

"What do you mean?"

"Demons…some are conjured, some rise of their own volition, some are born. Some are named and walk among us like men."

"Like werewolves."

"Yes. They cloak themselves in the guise of humanity. These are the beasts that occupy my days," he said then slid a black and white photograph toward me, tapping on a man in the picture. The image was of a gathering of lords and ladies. There was one man in the assembled group whose eyes glowed bright white.

"What I saw was more satyr than man," I said then went on to describe the creature.

Agent Hunter frowned. He rose and went to the bookshelf, grabbed a book, then sat beside me once more, sliding his seat close to mine. When he did so, I realized he must have washed up when he re-dressed. To my great delight, I caught the heavy scent of cologne with a hint of cinnamon. I inhaled deeply then let out a slow breath.

"Very strange," Agent Hunter said as he leafed through the book. "Conjured, perhaps. In which case we must hunt the mage, not the monster. But if he loosened himself from the Otherworld for some purpose, then he has a goal he will fulfill before he returns."

"Returns?" I said, turning to look at Agent Hunter, eyeing the light smattering of freckles on his nose and cheeks. They were…charming.

To my surprise, Agent Hunter was looking closely at me. His studied my face. "Your eye," he said, nodding to my mooneye. "Do you—I hope you don't mind me asking—but can you see from the eye at all?"

I nodded. "Some. Shapes, really. And some colors, but more like the glow of color than anything sharp. I'm told I'm quite lucky to have use of it at all."

Insecure thoughts swept over me. I had been considered very pretty—a sweet, pixie-like face, dark eyes, long black hair—before the injury. I knew I wasn't attractive anymore. On good days, I didn't think about it at all. On bad days, I knew I looked like a freak. I shifted in my seat.

"Sorry," Agent Hunter said. "I don't mean to pry. I had a tutor who had a mooneye. But he…well, he claimed he could see fairies because of it. I just wondered if you—"

"See fairies? No." Well, except for Lily Stargazer's

clockwork fairy, but that was different. "But I sometimes see…something."

"Something?"

"Enough of something that it helps me with the job," I said with a smile.

Agent Hunter grinned at me then turned back to the book. "I wish we could all see something. As for our demon problem, I was mentioning that a demon will often return once their goal is met. What kind of demon they are will often help us determine their goal. See if you recognize any of these," he said, flipping to a chapter in his book that contained drawings of genuinely hideous beasts. While the monster I'd tracked was fearsome, I was happy I didn't recognize any of those in the tome.

"A goal," I mused as Agent Hunter turned the pages. "I think I have a lead there. Strange as it may sound, I believe the demon is leaving a calling card. At the home of the first child who was abducted, a pear was left behind. Miss Anderson's father found a colly bird in her room. And the guttersnipes found some golden rings. In fact, our initial intel was completely wrong. Nine children have been abducted so far, not four."

"Nine!"

I nodded. "The little street rats who work the Strand were overlooked."

Agent Hunter frowned. "And likely they didn't make a report." He closed the book and set it aside. "From what you're saying, it's none of these then. Let me see," he said then rose and went to his bookshelf once more.

As he searched, I eyed over the table. A stack of his mail was lying there, including a Christmas postcard from someone with lovely feminine penmanship. I slid the note toward me to get a better look:

Dearest Edwin, we sincerely hope you can join us at Rushwood Hall for Christmas dinner. Most Sincerely, Eloise May and the Walcroft Family

Hell's bells. I knew it.

"Ah, perhaps this one," Agent Hunter said, pulling a book from the shelf.

Feeling guilty for snooping, I flipped the card over, pretending I hadn't read every word and wasn't currently stewing in a fit of jealousy.

When I did, however, I was shocked. There, on the face of the Christmas postcard, was the image of the demon I'd seen the night before.

Gasping, I stood. I lifted the postcard and stared at it.

"What is it?" Agent Hunter's eyes went to my hands. "Oh. Yes. The Walcrofts. I still haven't found an excuse to get out of that invitation."

"No, it's not that. Sorry about the unfortunate invite.

Why don't you come to dinner with me and my grand-mère on Christmas instead? This. It's this. It's him," I said, pointing to the image on the card.

The image of a giant, shaggy demon with horns, yellow eyes, cloven feet, and a forked tongue had been printed on the card. On his back, he carried a basket, a screaming child inside. Around his feet were Christmas packages, dolls, and toys. The card read: "Be Good! Krampus is Coming."

"I'd love to join you and your grand-mère. Thank you very much. Is that Krampus? You saw Krampus?" Agent Hunter said, taking the card from my hand. "You're sure? Absolutely sure?"

"Positive. He wears jingle bells on his green cloak and smells of peppermint. He looks exactly the same, down to the basket."

"Krampus has never manifested in London before. You said nine children have been taken so far?"

I nodded.

"It's almost Christmas. If we don't find these children before then—" Agent Hunter began.

"Then Krampus will take them back to the Otherworld with him. The children—Tobias, Lucas, Tom, and the little street rats—were all very naughty children. And little Elizabeth is more spoiled than Princess Helena. He's collecting some of the naughtiest children in London."

The color drained from Agent Hunter's face.

Grabbing me by my hand, he led me to the wall where a map of London was displayed. "Tell me again. Show me where were the children taken," he said.

"The Strand. Starting around Saint Clement Danes. Here," I said, pointing to the Browns' address. "Then at the orphanage, Waterloo—or thereabouts—near the Lyceum, the Alperstein', who I have not yet met, then last night here," I said, pointing.

Agent Hunter grabbed a pen from the table and marked on the map. We both stood and stared. Krampus was working the Strand, but his path was leading him directly to Buckingham.

"You tracked him to Saint James Park," Agent Hunter said stiffly as a terrible realization washed over both of us.

"Yes. Lost him near the lake."

"I need to send a messenger to Her Majesty. The Princess…"

Agent Hunter was right. If Krampus was hunting naughty children, then Princess Helena had to be his ultimate prize. The Queen's ill-tempered daughter's behavior was renowned. Newspapers and cartoon pamphlets joked about the princess. There wasn't a person in London who didn't know about her rotten behavior.

I nodded.

"We need to find his lair. We need to work the Park. He must be vanquished, sent back to Hell before nightfall tonight. But we need to find the other children first. Let me send some messages then get into uniform."

"Of course."

There was a knock on the door. "Breakfast, sir?" the butler called, pushing a cart loaded with food and a pot of hot tea.

"Clem—Agent Louvel, please, enjoy your breakfast. I'll get the messages out and join you in a bit. In the meantime, this will prove useful," he said, pulling yet another book from the shelf and handing it to me. He then hurried out of the room.

Clearing a spot at the end of the table, the butler set out my breakfast then left.

I sat down at the table, poured honey and slipped a bit of lemon into my tea, then took a sip. Perfection. I stared at the beautiful meal before me. My mouth watered at the heaps of eggs, ham, potatoes, scones, clotted cream, and jam. At the sight of all the food, I could barely focus on thoughts of Krampus, demons, and the poorly behaved Princess Helena.

But then another realization slowly washed over me.

I had invited Agent Hunter to Christmas dinner.

And he had said yes.

CHAPTER 10
Edwin & Clemeny

My belly full of ham, tea, and scones slathered in strawberry jam and clotted cream, I found my way back to Agent Hunter's chair by the fireplace. With his book in hand, I settled in. I flipped open the book to the title page: *A Guide to Wood Sprites, Elves, and Holiday Hobgoblins* by S. Rossetti. Inside the book, I found a bookplate indicating that the tome had at one time belonged to Horace Walpole and the library at Strawberry Hill House. It wasn't the first time I had heard that name and place associated with the preternatural. Mister Walpole was said to be very interested in the occult, and the current resident of the home, the Countess Waldegrave, was no different. I flipped to the table of contents then turned the yellowing pages to the section titled *Holiday Hobgoblins*. Therein, the author covered all manner of supernatural creatures associated with holidays. There was a hefty chapter on old Celtic Yule lore, the magical uses of mistletoe, the birth of Santa Claus—and the difference between him and Father Christmas—and Krampus.

I skimmed the pages, but suddenly my eyes felt very heavy. I slipped off my boots, curling my feet underneath me, and read.

Krampus, it seemed, was a well-known demon from the Alps, but he had been spotted in many regions throughout the world during the holidays. Early observers had incorrectly connected him to the Celtic god Cernunnos. Instead, he was an Otherworld creature who walked the mortal realm during the days leading up to Christmas. But conditions had to be right for him to enter the mortal realm. Wickedness, particularly in children, created dark energy which allowed him to enter the…the…

⊙ RM ⊙

"Agent Louvel," a soft voice called. Someone gently shook my shoulder. "Clemeny."

I inhaled deeply. Cinnamon.

Wait, did he just call me Clemeny?

My eyes fluttered open. I was still sitting in the chair by the fireplace, but I was covered by a heavy quilt. The sunlight streaming in through the window told me it was after dawn.

Agent Hunter, dressed in his formal uniform, stepped back. He smiled at me.

"I'm sorry to wake you. I don't think you've slept in more than a day, and probably little before that, but we need to get on the case."

Trying to wake up, I looked from him then around the room. Another chair had been pulled near the fire. A book sat on the seat, an empty cup of tea on the table beside it. Had he been sitting here with me?

"Sorry, sir. I—"

"Edwin," he said.

"Sorry?"

"Please, call me Edwin. At least, when the other agents are not around."

"Oh. Thank you…Edwin." *Oh my god, what is happening?*

He nodded. "I've sent messages to the palace, ordered increased patrols. I also sent word to Agent Fox, asking him to interview the Alpersteins and send in a report. You and I will head to Saint James Park. If my hunch is right, we will find the demon's portal there."

Still trying to master the fluttering in my heart, I refocused. "Yeah. Okay. All right. So, if silver doesn't harm the creature, what do you use?"

Agent Hunter—*Edwin*—motioned for me to follow him to the table where a wooden case was sitting.

"Before I was promoted, I worked in the field. I assume you already heard."

"Just rumors. But that's how I knew to come to you." There had been a lot of rumors about Agent Hunter's work before he became lead agent at Shadow Watch, but one tale persisted. Edwin Hunter was the best demon hunter in the realm.

He released the latches on his wooden case. Inside were vials of holy water, silver crucifixes, bags of dried herbs, a few clockwork devices I did not recognize, a bible, two unmarked journals that looked incredibly old, a dagger with a wooden blade, and a stake. "I think we'll find the right tool for the job."

"I really need one of those."

"Well, Christmas is coming."

I chuckled.

"First, we need to find the demon's lair. Shall we go hunting?"

Smirking, I nodded.

Agent Hunter closed up his demon hunting case, and we headed outside.

CHAPTER 11
Saddle Up

I half-expected Agent Hunter would have a fancy new auto, one of those disdainful coal or steam-powered contraptions that seemed to be taking London by storm. Instead, I found his horse saddled outside. The beast I had borrowed from the palace guard perked up when he saw me.

"Yes, I am here to take you home," I told the beast, patting him on the neck. I slipped into the saddle.

Agent Hunter mounted, securing his box behind him, and we headed off in the direction of the park.

It was still very early in the morning. There was a chill in the air, and a light dusting of snowflakes covered the ground. The delicious scents of gingerbread and sugar cookies perfumed the air outside a bakery. The shop fronts were decorated for the holidays. Green and red silk gowns, bonnets trimmed with holly, and other elegant frocks were on display in the windows. One shop used a zeotrope to show moving images of Santa in his sleigh flying around the holiday window scene. Other stores offered colorfully decorated Christmas crackers or ornaments for the newly popular Christmas tree. It seemed that whatever Her Majesty deemed festive and fashionable was suddenly becoming a tradition.

We rode across the city to the palace stables not far from Trafalgar Square and just outside Saint James Park.

As we approached, we earned the attention of two soldiers who gave us a hard look and then came our way.

"You there. Why do you have a guardsman's horse?" one man called.

Agent Hunter pulled his badge from inside his jacket and flashed it at the men. "There's no need for tone, gentlemen."

Both men paused, the more outspoken one eyeing me over.

"You're Agent Louvel?" he asked.

"Yes," I replied. "And this is Agent Hunter."

"Agents," the outspoken man said as he eyed us warily.

I slid off the horse and, taking it by the reins, led it to the man. "With my thanks and apologies," I said, handing over the lead.

"No need, Agent."

"We'll be investigating nearby today. I need to lodge my horse," Agent Hunter said.

"The stable master is in the office," one of the guards said, pointing.

With a curt nod, Agent Hunter led his horse in that direction. I followed along. When we arrived at the office, however, we could see through the window that the stable master was already engaged. A distraught stable hand was explaining something in an animated way. The stable master, who'd barely put down a paper he was reading, was trying to dismiss the worried man.

Agent Hunter tied his horse to a post. Without waiting for an invitation, he opened the stable master's door and entered. I waited just outside.

"It's just not like Nawali. He would never run off like this."

"Enough," the man said, his voice thick with irritation. "Don't make excuses for him. We both know that boy is always up to pranks. He'll turn up later today."

Agent Hunter cleared his throat. Both men turned to look.

"You're dismissed, Josiah," the stable master said.

The stable hand exited, his face showing a fit of fear and frustration. He headed back toward the stables. Agent Hunter started grilling the stable master, who was now standing, his attention restored. I went after the stable hand.

"Sir," I called.

The man did not stop.

"You there. Stable hand."

The man paused. He looked back. Seeing me, he lowered his eyes. "Sorry, my lady. I didn't realize you were calling me."

Because I'd called him sir. "No need to apologize. Agent Louvel. What's your name, sir?"

"Josiah."

"You were trying to tell the stable master someone is missing, am I right? Who has gone missing?"

"A stable boy. Nawali. He headed out this morning before dawn to feed and water the horses, and I can't find the boy anywhere. His grain buckets were sitting in the middle of the stable like the boy just vanished into thin air."

"This morning?"

"Yes. Before dawn."

My heart skipped a beat. "Show me where you found the grain pails."

"Yes, Agent," he said then motioned for me to follow.

Long rows of stalls housed regal looking beasts. Everything was neatly kept. Guards were milling around, getting their mounts ready for the day.

"How many people are on guard here early in the morning? When Nawali was out?" I asked.

"None, really. There are guards in the yard, but no one would be foolish enough to try to steal from the stables. They'd be shot on sight."

If anyone actually saw them. "When did you realize the boy was missing?"

"He always gets up before me, so I didn't think anything of it. But I heard the horses. They were riled up about something, snorting and whinnying, kicking their pen doors and walls. I came out to see what was the matter. I found the pails but no boy."

"I heard the stable master say the boy is a prankster."

"He is. But he has a good heart. At times, he takes his jests too far, that's all. Another hand was hurt recently as a result of Nawali's pranks. The stable master is not happy with him right now."

I frowned then followed Josiah to the far end of the stable, which just so happened to be situated across the street from Saint James Park.

"Here," the man said.

I scanned all around. The horses were standing at the back of their stalls, their eyes wide as they breathed in deeply. I looked all around for some sign of the beast. A soft breeze blew through the barn, stirring up the scents of hay, manure, and…peppermint?

"Do you smell that?" I asked the man.

"Sorry, Agent. The barn always—"

"No. Not that…on the breeze, there's something odd—"

"Peppermint."

Hell's bells. I had chased the beast away from one victim only for him to find an alternative closer to the park. I hadn't saved anyone, only changed the target.

Josiah bent and picked up a wooden box next to a stack of bales of hay. He opened the lid and looked inside, a perplexed expression on his face.

"What is it?" I asked.

Opening the box wide, he turned it so I could see. Inside were what looked like small flutes. They were very short with only one opening at the top.

"Pipes…kazoo, actually," the man said. "Like we play back home." He picked one up and blew through it. It made a rattling buzzing sound. "Nawali must have bought them. There's enough here for all the boys."

I counted the pipes in the box. There were ten. "May I keep those for the time being?" I asked.

Josiah nodded then handed the box to me.

"Agent Louvel?" Agent Hunter—*Edwin*—called.

"Sir," I said, turning to him. My eyes lingered on his for a long moment, my lips twitching to a smile which Agent Hunter echoed. Realizing that Josiah was looking at me, I reined in my grin then relayed everything Josiah had told me and what he had found.

Agent Hunter listened, his manner stiff and formal, a countenance I'd grown accustomed to in meetings. But I'd seen a brief glimmer of the real man behind that formal posture, and he was everything I had ever dreamed he would be.

"Thank you, Josiah. We shall see to the matter," Agent Hunter said.

"Thank you, sir. I had heard some children had gone missing, that's why I was so worried. I tried to tell the stable master. I never thought anyone would care about a stable boy. Why steal him?"

"We'll sort it out and bring him home," I reassured Josiah.

"Thank you, Agent. He's a foolish little boy, but he is dear to me."

I set a reassuring hand on the man's shoulder. "We'll do our very best. And we will also note in our report that your superior dismissed his disappearance," I said with a wink.

He smiled again. "Thank you, Agent," he said then headed back to the stables.

"Ten pipers piping," I said, showing the box to Agent Hunter.

He nodded then opened his case. He pulled out an odd-looking device that he held by a handle. He turned a windup key on the base. The device opened to reveal meters and lights inside. Keeping it in front of him, he swept it around, scanning the ground. The invention clicked as it worked, ticking more loudly in some places than others.

"Will you hold out the box of flutes, please?" he asked.

I nodded.

When the device was waved over the box, it began clicking loudly and a red light started blinking.

"What is that?" I asked.

"A very talented tinker found a way to track preternatural vibrations."

"So, it's like a bloodhound for the unnatural?"

Agent Hunter laughed as he swept the thing all around the exit of the stables. "Indeed," he was saying when the device went off once more. "And here is our trail. Shall we begin the hunt?"

"Lead the way," I said with a smirk, my admiration growing for Edwin ten-fold. If this kept up, I'd end up being the one to propose to him.

CHAPTER 12
Duck Island

We followed the trail as indicated by the clockwork device into Saint James Park. As we walked, guilt nagged at me. I thought I had saved a child, but instead, I had merely led the beast to find another, closer, victim. We needed to get this creature in hand. Immediately.

I kept an eye out as Agent Hunter moved through the park, his device leading us toward the lake.

"The tinker who made this device, who is he?" I asked.

"He's associated with the Rude Mechanicals."

Somewhere in the echelons of power above me, a group known as the Rude Mechanicals governed all the strange and unusual happenings in our realm. They had a direct line to Her Majesty and through my superiors, directed our agency. Who, exactly, they were, none of us actually knew. "Interesting."

"I've met him only a few times. I'm not sure what he does for the agency, exactly, but he is very good with such devices. I've delivered some intel to him at a pub in Sherwood on more than one occasion. He was always working on his devices while he was there. He was very interested in my work. He made this device for me."

"Get a name?"

"Robin something."

"Robin…in Sherwood?"

Agent Hunter laughed. "You suppose he gave me a pseudonym?"

I grinned "Maybe."

The device led us to an arched bridge leading from the central grassy area of the park to the small island commonly known as Duck Island.

We stopped at the foot of the bridge. The gate was closed. I crouched down and looked at the snow and ice thereon. I spotted cloven hoofprints.

I pointed. "There. Aren't arched bridges a common passageway for demons?"

"Yes. Let's have a look," he said. He bent down and opened his case, pulling out a sharp stake.

"Stakes? I thought those only worked on fangs. They work on demons?" I asked.

"Pins them down but doesn't vanquish them. Just

like your silver bullets, stakes will wound but won't necessarily kill," he said, seeing my gun was already drawn.

He unlatched the gate. The small island in the middle of the park was set aside for the conservation of waterfowl, thus earning it the name Duck Island. There was a little cottage on the island. As we passed over the pinnacle of the bridge, I scanned all around. The tracks led across the bridge and onto the island. The demon had not stopped at the crest of the bridge.

"Not a crossroads demon," Agent Hunter said, eyeing the footprints leading toward the cottage. His clockwork device still clicking madly, we followed the hoofprints onto the island. Moving quickly and quietly, we trailed the beast's steps to the small cottage. The tiny house, which was mainly used by scholars and conservationists, was abandoned for the winter.

"The beast…it's only been seen at night?" Agent Hunter asked in a whisper as we approached the quaint gingerbread style cottage.

I nodded.

"It must return to the Otherworld at dawn."

Agent Hunter signaled to me, and we sneaked up to the door.

Feeling a swell of self-consciousness, I pulled off my eyepatch and shoved it into my pocket. If there was a demon inside, I wanted to see him with both of my eyes. I really didn't want Agent Hunter staring at my mangled face, but I didn't have a choice. I needed to do the job right, which meant I needed my eye. And, besides, he'd called me Clemeny. That had to count for something, didn't it?

Agent Hunter glanced at me, his eyes briefly scanning my face, then set his hand on the door latch.

I readied my gun in front of me.

Motioning to me, and on the count of three, he opened the door.

My gun held in front of me, I stepped into the dark space.

Everything was perfectly still. Sunbeams showed through the window, dust motes floating through the air. The hair on the back of my neck rose. There was a smell of peppermint on the cool air. My good eye—used to working in the dark—quickly adjusted. As I scanned the room, my other eye spotted something in the hearth.

I edged deeper into the room, Agent Hunter following behind me. I moved toward the massive stone fireplace as Agent Hunter checked the adjoining rooms. On a table near the fireplace were cookie crumbles and shredded silvery paper and ribbons from Christmas crackers. The tiny gifts, which popped when you opened them, were usually filled with chocolates, cookies, or small gifts. The beast, it seemed, had enjoyed his share.

The floorboards creaked as Agent Hunter canvassed the other rooms. I squinted, looking more closely at the hearth. My good eye told me that the hearth was cold. But my mooneye saw green fire.

I cleared my throat, bracing myself to use his name once more, then called, "Edwin?"

"Clemeny? What is it? Have you seen something?"

"Point your device here," I said, motioning to the fireplace.

Agent Hunter knelt beside me, his device in front of him. The machine clicked quickly, the light blinking rapidly.

"How did you know?"

"I see...fire."

"Where?"

"Here," I said, waving my hand through the green flames. The heat felt strange—there, but not there all at once. "Green flames."

Edwin squinted at the unseen—at least to him—hellfire. "This is the portal then. Can you see anything beyond?"

I stared into the dark. At first, I saw only the unholy fire. Closing my right eye, my good eye, allowed me to see more. I could just barely make out shapes of something or someone moving on the other side. I shook my head. "There's something just out of sight."

Agent Hunter rose then offered me a hand up. "We

must trap him here. We must trap him and get the children out while the gate to the otherworld is still visible."

"But how?"

Agent Hunter tapped his demon hunting box. "I have an idea."

CHAPTER 13
Of Sacramental Oil, Honey, and Lemon

Trapping a demon took significantly more work than shooting a werewolf. Of course, hunting werewolves—especially when they were in wolf form—was merely a matter of being fast, smart, and hitting the target. Easier said than done.

Agent Hunter and I parted ways so he could make a report at the palace and inform Her Majesty of the dangers just outside her doorstep, while I went back into the city to Westminster Abbey.

"Sacramental oil?" the young priest asked, looking at me as if I had grown two heads. "Madame, we don't make it a habit of giving away such items. You need permission from my superiors."

"Then give me someone superior to talk to."

The young priest huffed then eyed my clothing.

"And just what does an air jockey need with sacramental oil?"

"I'm no air jockey, you foolish, prating knave. Bring me someone else to talk to."

In a huff, the priest left.

Left to my own devices, I wandered around the tombs of the kings and queens as I waited. I eyed the tomb of fat old Henry VIII. Something about the voluptuous and self-important king always intrigued me. And I half wondered, not for the first time, how long knowledge of the underbelly of our realm had been known to our monarchs.

I heard the sound of footsteps and the swish of robes coming toward me. Someone cleared their throat.

"Are you the young lady asking for the oil?"

I turned to find a very tall priest looking at me down the length of his nose.

"Yes. One bottle should do the trick."

"And what do you need it for?"

I pulled out my badge.

The man made the sign of the cross. He frowned at me. "I'll get you what you need, then you must leave this holy place."

Well, at least *he* knew who I was. "Very well."

The man turned on his heel and hastily departed.

"What do you make of that, Hank?" I asked King Henry.

"The priests are paranoid," a voice answered from behind me. "They spend all their lives worshipping the unseen then fear those who face it head on."

I turned back to find an old woman standing there. She was tying her bonnet on.

"You think so?"

She nodded. "Know it. Good luck to you, Agent. And Happy Christmas."

"Same to you," I said, grinning at the woman. Whomever she was, she was either very wise or had encountered someone from the agency before. At least someone in this city understood what we were about.

I turned back to the king, studying his tomb as I waited.

"So, who was your favorite wife?" I whispered. "Promise I won't tell."

No answer. Of course.

It was not long thereafter that I heard the slap of leather on the marble floors and the same familiar swish of cloth.

"Here you are," the tall priest said, holding out a glass bottle to me.

"And you're very sure it has been properly anointed?"

"Yes, Agent. Very certain."

I took the bottle from his trembling hand. "Her Majesty thanks you."

The man huffed, made the sign of the cross once more, then disappeared into the back.

I turned and headed back outside. Seemed no one at Westminster had much to say today.

(RM)

I MET AGENT HUNTER MIDAFTERNOON AT A NEARBY teahouse. The London streets were bustling with pre-Christmas merriment. Everywhere I went, people were hurrying past with packages, vendors were selling geese—and the fashionable turkey like the Yankees ate, another trend the Queen had started—plum pudding, and all manner of baked goods. The teahouse where we had agreed to meet was busy. I spotted Agent Hunter in the back. He rose when I joined him at the table, pulling out my chair. He really did have the breeding of a man beyond his current employment. Was there blue blood in his veins?

"I took the liberty of ordering us a pot of spiced tea and plowman's platters. Will that be all right for you?"

"Yes. Thank you," I said, slipping into the seat. When was the last time I had been anywhere with a man? A show? A stroll? A...anything? Aside from skulking around with Quinn, I realized my last outing had been with Lionheart at The Mushroom. I almost laughed at the absurdity of the idea.

"Were you able to get the oil?" Agent Hunter asked.

I nodded. "Oil, delivered via a very bitter priest with a very bitter attitude."

Agent Hunter chuckled. "Where did you procure it?"

"Westminster."

"Ah, that explains the attitude."

"How so?"

"Yes, well, I believe they assisted Agent Rose on a case not long ago, some doings with a nest of vampires. Since then, Westminster has been less than inclined to help the Society."

"They should thank us for vanquishing devils in their very midst."

"They should, but they don't. Most of the time, they only vaguely understand what we are doing, which is better for all of us."

"Here you are, sir. Ah, and your lovely wife," said a very plump woman with red cheeks and an equally red apron. She set down our plates and cups.

Agent Hunter opened his mouth to clarify but thought better of it.

"And cream. And sugar. And honey. I know your husband said you prefer your tea with honey and lemon, but this tea is spiced. I brought orange slices instead. Can I bring you anything else?"

"No, thank you," Agent Hunter said.

It pleased me to no end that he knew how I took my tea. Was he always so observant?

Pulling out some papers, Agent Hunter said, "I received a report from Agent Fox."

"On Harry Alperstein? The other boy who went missing?"

He nodded. "Disappearance follows the same pattern with one exception. There is no window in the room."

"Then how did it get in?"

Agent Hunter drew his chair a little closer to mine and unfolded a sketch of the room Agent Fox had provided. We studied the drawing, our heads close together. Once more, I caught the slightest scent of cinnamon. Heaven.

"The hearth," Agent Hunter said, tapping his finger on the drawing. "It can travel through the hearth if it must."

"Then it could show up anywhere, especially now that it knows it's being hunted. That complicates matters."

"We must take him down tonight."

I set the bottle of oil in front of Agent Hunter. "Just tell me what to do."

Lifting the teapot, Agent Hunter poured me a cup of tea then added a slice of orange.

"First, you must have a cup of spiced holiday tea *with orange*," he said with a playful chuckle.

I smiled at him. "Thank you, husband," I said, reaching out to squeeze his hand in mock playfulness. To my surprise, however, he set his other hand on mine.

"Anytime."

And then, I might have swooned. Just a little.

CHAPTER 14
Portals, Peppermint, and Ladies Dancing

In the hours before dusk, Agent Hunter and I readied the trap. We would need to act quickly. The beast must be captured near the hearth and forced to keep the portal open if we wanted to recover the children. There was great risk if we failed, and we both knew it.

We readied the room and lay in wait as the sun went down.

Crouched behind a chair near the hearth, I eyed Agent Hunter's hiding place. Hunting demons was nothing like hunting wolves. At least they would fight you out in the open.

There was a whoosh of cool air then green fire erupted in the fireplace. I heard jingle bells, and the smell of peppermint seemed to overwhelm the room. I steeled my nerve and waited.

I heard soft crying in the distance. The children? My heart ached.

The whole room seemed to shake as the beast stepped into the room. I watched his cloven hooves from my hiding spot.

One step.

Then another.

And another.

I rose quickly, struck a match, and tossed it at the invisible ring of sacramental oil on the floor. A moment later, the whole circle caught fire.

Confused, Krampus turned and looked at me, his yellow eyes narrowing as he took in the trap. He sneered, his forked tongue shooting out at me.

Agent Hunter emerged from the darkness, his leather journal in his hand. At once, he began reciting an incantation in Latin to exorcise the demon. If this worked, the demon would be immobilized, and we could force it to do our will. At least, that was what Agent Hunter had said. It really was so much easier to shoot something with a silver bullet.

Pulling my knife, I stepped back as Krampus looked from me to Agent Hunter. His manner, the way he was moving, told me something was very wrong.

The demon laughed. "Do you think the new god's petty words can trap me? You fools."

The demon crouched then growled.

Agent Hunter spoke the incantation louder, but nothing was happening.

I looked back at the hearth. The green flame was beginning to extinguish.

"Edwin," I called in warning.

But I was too late.

The demon stepped out of the circle and lunged at Agent Hunter, slapping the book from his hand. Agent Hunter reacted quickly, pulling a wooden stake from his belt. The beast grabbed the stick. When he did so, the wood began to grow, new shoots, leaves, and branches rapidly appearing. The beast hit Agent Hunter on the head with the stake, which had turned into a club in the beast's grasp, then grabbed Agent Hunter by the neck of his shirt and flung him aside. Agent Hunter hit the wall hard, slumping to the ground.

My heart skipped a beat, my fury boiling over.

My dagger drawn, I lunged toward the beast, who took a swipe at me. Anticipating the move, I ducked low. The demon missed. Reaching out, I slashed at him, but I missed. I turned, pulling my pistol, and took aim.

With a long, clawed hand, the demon reached out and grabbed my arm. To my great shock, the beast cried out in pain when his hand landed on the vambraces I always wore to protect me from the nipping jaws of werewolves.

He let go.

I yanked my arm back, took aim, and shot.

But the beast fled. The monster ducked then raced out of the room. I'd missed.

I ran to Edwin who was only half-conscious, blood leaking from a cut above his eye. "Go," he whispered. "Go."

Nodding, I turned and ran outside.

Krampus hurried off into the night. I could see his hulking shadow and heard the jangling of bells. In the distance, the palace guards' hounds started baying. They smelled the danger.

The monster fled through the park and turned toward Downing Street. I rushed after him, but the creature's cloven hooves carried him along with supernatural speed. It took everything I had to keep him in sight. I watched as the monster quickly scaled up the side of a building. Though the townhouses there had once been a popular home for the Chancellor of the Exchequer and other high positions, of late, the street was neglected. The official residences were rarely used. Alleys not far away were known for crime, prostitution, and other misdoings, not part of my normal beat.

Racing behind the creature, I climbed up a ladder then crawled up onto the rooftops behind him. The beast leapt from rooftop to rooftop, the moonlight illuminating his massive silhouette. I raced after him, pausing only to take another shot.

The creature ducked behind a chimney just in time. I saw a spray of brick dust.

Dammit.

The demon emerged once more, casting a glance back at me, his yellow eyes shining. He grinned, then jumped across the roof, and then slipped into a garret window at eleven Downing Street.

From inside the house, I heard a scream.

Racing behind the creature, I scrambled over the narrow pitch to the garret. The window was open. Taking a calculated jump, I slipped inside, my pistol ready. But there was no one in the room.

Once more, I heard someone yell. The sound came from the floor below. I raced down the dimly lit hallway and ran down the stairs. At the end of the stairwell, a man in his nightgown wearing a stocking cap appeared from inside one of the rooms. He was holding a lamp and staring at me like he'd seen the ghost from Mister Dickens' story.

Down the hallway in the opposite direction, a child screamed. I raced down the hall, the man hurrying behind me.

I pushed open the door in time to see Krampus holding a young boy, his clawed hand covering the child's mouth. The boy's eyes were wide with fear.

No. No, no, no.

Krampus glared at me. Then he turned his attention

to the small fireplace.

"Stop. Stop now, or I'll shoot," I said, taking aim.

With a wave of his hand, the beast called up a blaze of green fire in the fireplace.

"And kill the child? He deserves to die, rotten little boy," Krampus said.

"Arthur!" the man behind me called out in fear.

Without another thought, the beast jumped into the fireplace, dragging the boy along with him.

"No," I shouted. I leapt after them. I grabbed the child by the foot and pulled hard, trying to yank the boy out of the monster's grasp.

But then something came loose. The little boy slipped from my grip, and I stumbled. I landed on the floor in front of the hearth. The green fire dissipated. The portal sealed. I looked from the fireplace to the striped sock in my hand.

He had gotten away.

And I had lost the boy.

Sitting by the hearth in front of me was a wooden box. The lid was open. Inside were eleven tiny wooden ballerinas.

Eleven ladies dancing.

One to go.

And if we failed now, given who we figured the next target to be, it would cost Agent Hunter and me our heads.

CHAPTER 15
In a Heartbeat

My heart beating hard, I called for the local constables to take a full report, sent a runner to wake up Agent Fox to help, then raced back to the Duck House. I had a terrible vision that the sacramental oil had caught the entire house on fire, Edwin unconscious and surrounded by the flames. But when I got there, the fire was out and Edwin was sitting on the step outside, the leafy sprig that had once been a stake in his hand.

"Clemeny," he called, standing when he saw me. "What happened?"

I inhaled deeply. I had failed. Arthur Pembroke, the nephew of the Chancellor of the Exchequer, who had come to London to watch *The Nutcracker* and to enjoy some holiday revelry before returning to the countryside, was gone.

I shook my head. "I was too late."

"Another child?"

I nodded then explained what had happened.

Edwin sat back down. I slid onto the step beside him.

He handed me the branch. It looked like it had been freshly plucked from a spring forest. Even the leaves held the heavenly smell of spring.

"It's oak," Edwin said.

Frowning, I looked at the branch as I thought over what had happened.

"That creature…he is no demon," Edwin said. "If he was, we would have ended this tonight. No demon can escape a ring of sacramental oil. Not even the worst of them," he said then winced.

I dug a handkerchief from my pocket then turned to him. "You're bleeding," I told him. Holding his chin gently, I blotted the blood away. "Might need stitches." I tried to hold my hand steady, tried not to tremble. But being this close to him, this intimate, made the ember inside me spark into a full-fledged flame. I bit the inside of my cheek and willed myself not to say something completely ridiculous.

"No time. We need to…" he said, but then his voice trailed off.

I paused and looked at him, lowering the handkerchief.

He was staring at me, a soft expression on his face.

Is this really happening?

I loosened my grip on his chin then gently, moving carefully, I touched his cheek.

"I see the way you look at me," he whispered. "The way your mouth twitches with a smile at your thoughts." Reaching out, his finger trailed across my lips. "I wonder what you're thinking in those moments."

"Maybe it's better if you don't know."

"No. I want to know. I want to know if you're thinking the same thing I think when I look at you."

"Edwin," I whispered.

He leaned in toward me.

The baying of hounds sounded close by. A group of guards holding torches approached.

"Who's there?" a gruff voice called to us.

Edwin paused then exhaled regretfully. "Agents Hunter and Louvel."

My knees weak, somehow, I rose, as did Edwin. Standing side by side, we faced the palace guards, Agent Hunter's hand resting gently on the small of my back.

"Agents," the guard said. "What's the matter here?"

"Sir, will you please send one of your men? I need to speak to Her Majesty. Immediately."

CHAPTER 16
What Sir Gawain Knew

As Edwin and I walked to Buckingham, I tried to focus on the beast. If Krampus was not a demon, what was he? We needed to dive into the lore quickly. But the more I tried to think about Krampus, the more my thoughts returned again and again to the near-kiss. An almost kiss. A so-damned-close kiss. Hell's bells. He actually felt the same way about me? About me? That was impossible.

"The beast," Edwin said, also trying to divert attention away from the terrible tension that lay between us. "When it grabbed you, it yelped. Why?"

"He set his hand on my vambrace."

"Is it made of silver?"

"My vambraces are made of steel but coated in silver. The silver burns the wolves, but the steel helps to deflect bites."

"Good god," Edwin said with a laugh. "You really did deserve more than a goose for a bonus."

I grinned but thought over his point. "So was it the silver or the steel that affected him? And then there was the stake. It grew in the beast's grasp."

Agent Hunter stopped. "Faeries."

"Sorry?"

"Faeries. Well, more specifically, Unseelie. Dark fey. Steel burns faeries."

"That would also explain the branch."

"Krampus is not a demon at all. He is a dark fey creature."

"Now, how in the hell do we fight something like that?"

Edwin smiled. "I have an idea," he said and then headed into the palace where we were met by a footman who'd been expecting us.

"The library, please," Edwin told him.

"Of course, sir," the man replied then led us down a series of hallways.

I had been in the palace a few times in the past. It was as opulent as I expected. With tapestries, oil paintings, fine rugs, and polished floors, it was the picture of everything a palace should be. I tried not to let it over-impress me, but it was hard. The Queen and her family lived in wealth unlike anything I would ever know. What was remarkable about the palace, however, was how festively everything was trimmed. There must not be a sprig of evergreen in the forests nearby. Red bows, pine boughs, gold and silver ornaments, candles, and all manner of holiday finery adorned the rooms and halls. The footman led us to the library, closing a set of double doors behind us. Edwin went quickly to the stacks, his fingers drumming along the spines as he looked.

"Let me see. It should be right…here," he said, pulling a volume from the shelf.

"How did you know the book you wanted was there?" I asked.

"I…well…it's not important. Come. Take a look," he said, flipping open the book.

Coming to stand beside him, I looked down to see he was looking at a copy of the Arthurian tale of *Sir Gawain and the Green Knight*.

"Sir Gawain?"

Edwin nodded. "The beast put me in mind of something. It wasn't until we made the fey connection that I remembered. Have you ever read this poem?"

"Years ago."

"Sir Gawain is tested by a magical creature, a fey creature all in green, during the Christmas season. The creature comes to the court to play a Christmas game. The monster, the Green Knight, called into question the true virtue of Arthur's court. They fail miserably. Sir Gawain beheads the Green Knight, at Arthur's suggestion. But the monster

—magical as he is—puts his head back on and rides off, challenging Gawain to meet him a year later. Only then does Gawain defeat the knight…through his virtue."

"You think it is the same creature?"

"Yes. It is a faerie. Steel burned it. And the stake confirms it. Now we must consider how to vanquish it."

"But Gawain won by virtue alone. Our problem is the children. The lot of them lack virtuous qualities. How can we fix that?"

"Well, in the least, we know the monster's next—and last—target. He has been working toward the biggest offender all this time."

"Princess Helena."

Edwin nodded. "I think I know how to capture the monster. In the poem, Gawain wears a pentacle. It is described as having all the virtues of Christ, but it is also a symbol of the Druids. The pentacle is an ancient symbol and highly magical. I believe if we can get the beast into a pentacle, it will stop him."

"And then?"

"We must convince the beast to leave the portal to the Otherworld open to retrieve the missing children."

"How will we do that?"

"Bind him."

"Easier said than done. Bind him with what?"

"Mistletoe," a voice answered from the door.

We both turned to find Queen Victoria standing there.

"Your Majesty," Edwin said with a deep bow.

"Your Majesty," I echoed, curtseying deeply.

The queen turned to the footman following her. "I need a sack of mistletoe. Immediately. Have someone search the grounds. It must be trimmed with a silver blade. And only silver. Do you understand?"

"Yes, Your Majesty," the servant said then hurried off.

The queen closed the door behind her.

"Well, Edwin, I assume you failed to catch the beast tonight."

"We tried, Your Majesty. I falsely believed it was a demon I was hunting. It's not. It is an Unseelie."

Queen Victoria sighed heavily then crossed the room to join us, picking up the tome of *Sir Gawain and the Green Knight* that we were reading. "So you believe he is coming for Helena?"

"Yes, Your Majesty," Edwin said.

The queen looked over the book then set it down. She looked from Edwin to me. "Nice to see you again, Agent Louvel," she said, studying my face. She looked back at Edwin. "Do you remember Master Griffiths? From Cottingley? He had a mooneye too."

I wanted to sink into the floor.

Edwin shifted uncomfortably then said, "I do. He could see fairies. Do you remember?"

Queen Victoria nodded. "I was always jealous. I begged to go to Master Griffiths's house, to his garden, so I could see them too. And you, Agent Louvel, since the incident, do you ever see fairies?"

"No, Your Majesty."

"Too busy hunting werewolves, I suppose. Do you and Sir Richard still have that situation in hand?"

"Yes, Your Majesty," I replied.

"Very good. Well now, you were talking about virtue. If I overhead you correctly, you believe a virtuous act may redeem my daughter and save the missing children. Is that right?"

"Yes, Your Majesty," Edwin said.

The queen sighed. "You know Helena is the most foul-tempered child in the land? Devoid of virtue and entirely selfish?"

"That is the reason, we believe, the beast was summoned here. All the children taken thus far are ill-mannered," I said. "But an act of virtue on the part of your daughter may undo the damage."

The queen crossed the room and slid the book back onto the shelf. "Very well. Let's give it a try. And if we cannot convince her, perhaps the beast will."

CHAPTER 17
Princess Helena

To say that Princess Helena, all of five years old, was spoiled, would be an understatement. First, the child would hear nothing from any of us on the matter of the missing children. Nor would she hear anything on the subject that a foul beast was going to come and haul her away.

"Fairy tales," the princess said dismissively. "No one will be coming through my chimney except Santa Claus to bring me exactly what I asked for. And not an item less," the princess informed the three of us.

"Helena," Her Majesty implored. "You are in grave danger. The agents are here to protect you, but you must do as they tell you."

"If I am in so much danger, then why don't we remove to Hampton?" she replied tartly.

"It doesn't matter where you go, Princess. The beast

will find you," I warned the child who turned and glared at me, her face crinkling as she looked me over.

"What happened to your face?" she asked.

"Helena," Queen Victoria scolded. "Do not be rude."

"It's all right," I said. "I was attacked by a werewolf. He scratched my face, and I nearly lost my eye."

Princess Helena snorted. "Werewolf? Another fairy tale? Pity. I bet you used to be pretty."

"That's quite enough," Queen Victoria said sternly. "Time for you to go to bed."

I bit the inside of my cheek and said nothing. The princess was right. Before the scratch, I had been pretty. Before the scratch, I'd at least had a chance to find a suitor. But now… I couldn't bear to look at Edwin. How could he ever really be interested in a woman like me? It was clear that Edwin knew the queen personally. They'd shared a tutor. That meant he'd lived, at least at some point, in the palace. Was he a Lord's son? I hardly knew. But what I did know was that a well-born man could hardly be seen on the arm of a disfigured Red Cape Society agent, particularly one below him in rank. Whatever that kiss might have been, I was suddenly glad it was a near miss. The princess simply said what everyone else was thinking. Rude as it was, it was true. Hell, even Lionheart preferred Bryony Paxton over me. What made me think I had a chance with someone like Edwin Hunter?

Agent Hunter motioned to me, and we stepped outside while the queen fought her reluctant child into bed. I heard the princess pitch a tantrum as we waited.

"Clemeny, please don't think anything of—"

"It would be best if we stay close by tonight. We can get to work first thing in the morning. Do you think Her Majesty would oblige us?" I said, trying desperately to change the subject.

"Of…of course. I'll ask her."

"Very good. I'll head to the servant's area to see about the mistletoe. Queen Victoria is right. If there is anything that can ward faeries, Seelie, Unseelie, or even a tiny fey, it's mistletoe," I said then turned and walked away before Edwin could say anything else.

It was good we hadn't kissed. Seems even cruelty could sometimes be kind. The princess's sharp words were just the reminder I needed.

CHAPTER 18
Agent Louvel in the Library with the Lamp

Her Majesty was kind enough to let Edwin and me stay in the palace that night. She was doubly kind to ensure a maid brought me a proper dressing gown to wear that evening. I tossed and turned most of the night, trying to think of anything but the missed kiss. It had *nearly* happened in the heat of the moment. Between the moonlight and the soft snow, the magical time had called for a kiss. But the moment had also been fleeting. Surely, Edwin hadn't really meant anything by the look, the words, the touch.

Right?

Right?

Oh, hell's bells.

It must have been some time after midnight when I finally got tired of not sleeping. Pulling on the red velvet robe and slipping on a pair of soft slippers, my long black hair—save the white streaks—hanging loose, I headed back to the library. About six different servants intercepted me, but I managed to convince them to let me continue on my way. I needed to be ready for tomorrow, and I wasn't going to get that done in bed mooning over a missed kiss.

To my surprise, however, Edwin was already in the library. The poem was open in front of him, and he was sketching and taking notes in his journal. A number of other books lay on the table before him.

"Oh," I stammered, standing in the doorway, my smoldering lamp held out in front of me.

Edwin rose. "Clemeny," he said softly, crossing the room toward me. "I couldn't sleep either. Your lamp is smoking," he said, taking it from my hand and turning down the flame. "Come on. Let me show you something. Prince Albert was by earlier. We had a brandy, and he told me about the legends of Krampus in his home country. The beast is well known there, and the children always behave well enough to prevent evoking his ire. See here," Edwin said, sliding a couple of books across a table toward me as he took a seat.

I slid into the chair beside him. The books were in German, which I could not read, but I could clearly make out the engravings therein. Images of Krampus spanking naughty children or putting them in his basket filled the pages.

"How do they ward him off in Germany?"

"By encouraging good behavior, mostly. In truth, they haven't had a sighting of the beast in the material world for many years."

"Then their method must be working. The balance of virtue versus vice has tipped in London. That opened the portal."

Edwin nodded. "I believe we can ensnare the beast. We must draw him out, allow the princess to act as bait. We will draw the pentacle described in the poem under the rug before the fire. It will lock him in place."

"And the mistletoe?"

"We will use steel chains to bind him and a garland of mistletoe to seal the enchantment."

"Then we should start working on the garland."

"No need. Her Majesty has already seen to it."

"That's…surprising."

"Her Majesty is quite knowledgeable about Druidic lore."

"How so?"

"When we were children, we had a tutor who was a member of the Rude Mechanicals. We received quite the education."

"You…you were educated alongside Her Majesty?"

"I was a childhood playmate. My father was a Baronet, her mother's attaché."

"Oh," was all I could manage.

Wonderful. Not only was Edwin my superior in the agency, but he was also my superior in life. He wasn't just Lead Agent Edwin Hunter, he was Sir Edwin Hunter. What had I been thinking? I was a no one, a nothing. The only title I had was *Little Red.* Hell, I didn't even know who my parents were. There was no way he was really interested in me like that. Not possible.

"Tomorrow, we will prepare the princess's room. You're right that moving her won't help. But Prince Albert asked for a fleet of guards outside the door. Brute force, if nothing else, will be our last line of defense. Victoria will stay in the room with us."

"Is that wise? She is, after all, our Queen," I said, trying to distract myself from the emotional avalanche that wanted to overwhelm me.

"Helena is her daughter. Naughty though she may be, mothers love their children. And many times, the naughtier they are, the more the parent secretly loves them for it."

I wouldn't know.

"Do you…do you think the beast knows we suspect his next target?" I asked, willing my voice to be steady.

"I don't know. He knows we found his lair, and after last night, he will be wary."

I nodded.

A lull of silence fell between us. The unspoken

words hung so heavily in the air that I shifted uncomfortably in my seat.

"Clemeny," Edwin said gently.

I rose. "I think we have a plan. I should get some rest."

Edwin rose as well. "Are you certain? I mean, of course. Goodnight."

Taking my lamp, I headed back out of the library. I paused at the door and looked back at Edwin who was staring at me with such a forlorn expression that I almost rushed across the room to him.

Almost.

"Goodnight, Edwin."

He smiled then nodded. "Goodnight."

"Goodnight."

"Goodnight."

Good god, were there ever two more awkward people in the world? Grinning, I turned and left. Maybe, just maybe.

CHAPTER 19
Not Quite Milk and Cookies

We spent the following day getting ready. The rug in the princess's room was cleared, and we worked at drawing the pentacle underneath, reinforcing it with faerie warding. Faeries were slippery creatures. Though not part of my routine beat, I knew there were others who monitored their movements. A full troupe hadn't been spotted in London since the Frost Fair of 1814. But then it was the good faeries, the Seelie, whose Golden Troupe who had appeared. I had no idea when a dark creature from their world had last been seen. Perhaps it was Sir Gawain who'd last tangled with a boggart. But Gawain had won. Would we be able to do the same? Much depended on the princess, who didn't seem the slightest bit inclined to be helpful.

"Just look at this floor. Mother. Mother! Look what

they are doing to my floor," Princess Helena said with a stomp of the foot.

"They are doing it to protect you, my dear," Her Majesty reassured the child.

"Rubbish. They are ruining my Christmas, and you are letting them! How will I ever play with my new dolls in such mess? How will I try on my new dresses if they are here in my room? If they scare Santa Claus away with their occultism, I shall have them both hanged."

"Helena! Occultism? Please. Now, get what you've come for and let's go. We have guests to meet."

"You'll have to buy me a new rug. The bottom of this one will be completely ruined after this," the Princess said, snatching a red bow trimmed with beads from her dressing table before heading back to the hallway.

Queen Victoria paused to watch our work.

"Mother!" Princess Helena screamed from afar.

"I've gone through twelve governesses. Twelve," the Queen said to no one in particular then turned and followed the unruly child back outside.

When we were done, Edwin went to check in with the palace guard while I prepared the mistletoe. If worse came to worst, either Edwin or I would have to cross into the Otherworld to retrieve the missing children. If we didn't get the children out by the stroke of midnight, it would be too late. Once Christmas arrived,

Krampus would be gone, and his victims along with him.

I stared at the fireplace.

And if we were wrong, if Krampus did not come for the princess tonight, then another child would be lost. The rest of them too. But I had no doubt in my mind that Princess Helena had to be the target. She was the naughtiest child I had ever seen.

"Do you need anything?" a voice called from the door. I looked up to see Prince Albert standing there.

I curtseyed. "No, Your Highness."

He gave me a curt nod. "I understand you tracked the beast to the Duck House. My wardens tell me there is evidence of fire in the building."

"Yes. We tried to capture the beast there, but we were unsuccessful. Fire was involved, but ineffective."

"I wanted to rebuild that building anyway," he said with a thoughtful smile then looked from the drawing of the pentacle on the floor to me. "My wife tells me you and Agent Hunter are the best in your agency. My daughter is precious to me. We understand that the beast will come for her no matter where we go, what we do. My men will be here. We cannot let this monster have her. Do you understand? You must protect her. My daughter, my children, are everything to me."

"Yes, Your Highness. I do. I will protect her, or I will die trying."

The man nodded once more, and without another word, he left.

After he'd gone, I wondered then about the fierce love between a parent and child. If a parent could love their child no matter their temperament, love them with all their flaws, and love them fiercely, then how had I ended up on the steps at Saint Clement Danes?

CHAPTER 20
Why So Naughty?

It was very late when Her Majesty tucked Princess Helena into bed. The Queen lay down beside her.

"Princess," Edwin said, standing at the child's bedside. "Don't be afraid. Agent Louvel and I are here. We will protect you. And your father and his men will be stationed just outside the door. No matter what you see, don't be scared. We are all here to keep you safe."

"Scared? Of a boggart? Daft man. Only a bad person would try to scare a child on Christmas eve. Shame on you, sir. My mother should have you relieved of duty and stripped of title. See to it, Mother," the child said with a yawn then fell asleep.

I raised an eyebrow but said nothing.

Her Majesty shook her head. "Edwin, what should I do?"

"Now all we can do is wait."

The Queen looked down at the sleeping princess. "It is my fault," she said. "Despite my best efforts, I could never calm her temperament nor her tongue."

"Don't judge yourself so harshly, Your Majesty. Children often sprout in the opposite direction of their parents' care just to spite them," I said, hoping to comfort her.

"As I did," Edwin said with a smile that the Queen returned.

"And may we all thank God for that," she told Edwin with a soft laugh. "But she has put herself in danger. I fear for her," the Queen said as she brushed a stray strand of hair away from her daughter's face.

"We'll protect her," Edwin assured her.

Her Majesty laid her head back down then collected her child in her arms. To my surprise, the little princess sighed contentedly and wiggled deeper into her mother's embrace. While she had the mouth of a devil when she was awake, asleep, Princess Helena was the picture of sweetness.

I looked at Edwin, who nodded, and we took up our positions not far from the fireplace.

And then, we waited.

And waited.

The chime of a grandfather clock somewhere down the hall had just sounded eleven fifteen when the air in the room stirred like someone had opened a window. A cold breeze filled the room, a flurry of snowflakes whooshing out of the fireplace as green light filled the princess's chamber. I smelled the familiar scent of peppermint and heard the jingle of bells.

From my spot in the darkness, I saw the beast emerge.

His eyes were fixed on the princess's bed. He never even passed a glance our way.

Edwin moved out of the darkness. He nodded to me. I lifted the length of chain I was holding and threw the other end to Edwin. He caught it before the beast could even see what was happening and, working quickly, we ran toward one another, binding the chain around the monster.

Krampus howled angrily, and jerked at the chains that entangled him, but having stepped fully into the pentacle hidden under the rug, he was frozen.

"What is this? What is this?" the beast yelled.

The princess sat up in bed, the queen rising beside her, gathering her child protectively into her arms.

Princess Helena's eyes grew wide.

The monster laughed, tugging on the iron binds Edwin and I had wrapped around it.

"We know what you are now," Edwin said, rushing behind the beast to bind his wrists with the garland of mistletoe. Between the steel, the trap, and sacred herb, we had the monster right where we wanted it. "Now, you will leave the princess in peace, and you will release the children."

The monster laughed. "You will never get the children back. They belong to my world."

"Not until midnight, they don't," I said. "Release them," I said then pulled my gun, aiming it on the monster.

The beast snarled. "Go get them yourself, *Little Red*."

I glared at him.

"What children?" the princess demanded. "What children are they talking about?"

"The beast has kidnapped eleven children. You were intended to be the twelfth," the Queen explained.

While we had informed the haughty princess of all this before, apparently she hadn't listened. Maybe it hadn't seemed real until there was a seven-foot monster in her bedchamber.

At that, the princess stood up in her bed. "You! You nasty creature. How dare you capture my subjects? Where are they? Release them immediately."

Krampus laughed. "They are there, proud princess." He looked back at the fireplace. With a bob of his pointed chin, the portal opened wider. Though the portal was surrounded by green flames, we could see a cage in which all the children were trapped.

"The children," Victoria said with a gasp. She rose as if she was planning to go retrieve them herself.

"No, Your Majesty," Edwin said. "Stay with Clemeny and the princess. I'll go."

Krampus laughed. "Try it, foolish mortal."

"No, Edwin. Let me," I said then moved toward the fireplace. "I can see," I said, motioning to my mooneye.

Not waiting for him to reply, and not letting myself have a moment to think better of it, I moved toward the portal. To my surprise, however, I met with a barrier blocking my path. I couldn't break through.

Krampus laughed. "Who are you, werewolf hunter, to enter my world? You have the right blood, but you know nothing."

Frustrated, I turned and pressed my pistol into the beast's back. "Set those children free now. Silver may not burn you, but I'm guessing being shot at close range will smart a bit. Set them free. Now."

"If you kill me, and they will live among my court forever."

The princess hopped off her bed. In her long pink nightgown, she approached the beast. Edwin moved toward her.

"Let those children go," she told the monster.

"And why would I? My realm is for monsters, for children like them and *you*," Krampus said with a hiss.

Angry, the princess kicked the monster in the shin, making him laugh.

"You see," he said.

"If only a monster can enter your world then so be it!" the princess declared, and without another thought, she turned and ran straight into the fireplace and out of sight.

"Helena," Queen Victoria screamed which prompted the bedchamber door to open and a flood of soldiers, headed by Prince Albert, to appear in the room.

"Ready your weapons! Aim—"

"Stop," I called, stepping in front of the firing squad about take down the beast.

"Helena, Helena," Queen Victoria screamed, fighting against Edwin who was restraining the queen as she struggled to get to the fireplace.

"Agent Louvel, Agent Hunter, explain yourselves," Prince Albert demanded.

"Sir, we need the beast alive to keep the portal open," I hastily explained as I looked down the barrel of a dozen muskets.

"Helena," Victoria called.

I looked back toward the fireplace. The image on the other side was distorted. I saw movement. The green firelight flickered.

Once more, a cold breeze whipped through the room. A whirlwind of snowflakes blew across the bedchamber.

"This way. Right this way. Everyone hold hands.

Hang on tight, and don't be afraid. Right this way," I heard Princess Helena say.

Gasping, I stared.

Hand-in-hand, the princess led the children out of the fireplace, out of the Otherworld, and away from Krampus.

"There. Go to my father. There," she said, ushering each child toward Prince Albert. I recognized little Elizabeth from the miniature of her that her father had worn. The guttersnipes were well-marked by their clothing, as was little Nawali the stable boy. I counted as each child rushed out and ran to the prince. Eleven children and the princess. Twelve in all. All safe and sound.

Princess Helena turned and faced down the monster.

"Go back to your realm where you belong. You are forbidden from entering our world ever again. Do you understand?"

"Brave little princess, it hardly matters what I understand. Do *you* understand why I have come? All of you?"

The terrified children hiding behind the prince nodded vehemently.

Krampus turned to the princess. "And you?"

"Point taken. Now be gone, monster," she said.

Hands shaking, Queen Victoria came to stand in front of Krampus. Her large, piercing eyes met his.

"May mistletoe bind you," she said, sketching an arcane symbol in the air before her. "And let mistletoe ward you," she said, drawing another symbol in the ether. "Wherever the sacred plant is present, you will not pass," Queen Victoria added, finishing off her…spell? "Tell the Unseelie Queen that if I find any of her underlings in my realm once more, she will face my wrath," she added in a low, dark whisper then motioned to Edwin and me.

Grabbing the beast, we pushed him back through the portal.

The fireplace sealed once more just as the clock in the hallway struck twelve.

Princess Helena smiled. "Happy Christmas, one and all."

CHAPTER 21
Sinners Reconciled

Hark! The herald angels sing
Glory to the new-born King
Peace on earth and mercy mild
God and sinners reconciled

Though it was midnight, the entire royal household was awake. The children sang as they gathered around the large Christmas tree in the royal family's parlor. Princess Helena had spent the last half hour trying to convince her brothers and sisters that she was telling the truth about what had happened. Of course, they thought she was pulling a prank. I could see from the fire in the little princess's eyes that she was growing increasingly angry, but she managed to keep a lid on her anger. Seemed Krampus had taught her a lesson after all.

Messengers were sent to the families of the children

to inform them that their little ones had been recovered and could be safely retrieved from Buckingham.

"I will spread the fashion," Queen Victoria said, linking her arm with Edwin's. "Mistletoe has always been a favorite. I will decree it the most festive thing for families to keep a bundle of mistletoe in the home during the holidays."

"And how will you ensure they follow the fashion? Some will find it too pagan, remembering its Celtic roots," Edwin said.

Victoria snapped her fingers. "We'll tell them that if they spot their love standing near the mistletoe, they can snatch a kiss."

"We shall have a shortage of mistletoe in England," I said with a grin.

We all laughed.

Smiling, I looked at the children. While the families would soon arrive for Elizabeth, Tobias and the others, the poor street rats would not be so lucky.

"Your Majesty, some of the children are without homes, without families," I told her.

She nodded. "So I was informed. I have offered them places here. Always room for another page or stablehand."

My queen continually surprised me. I curtsied to her then crossed the room to Lucas and Tom, the boys from

Saint Clement Danes. Lucas stood with his arm linked around a girl's—presumably Bunny—waist.

"Boys," I said, nodding to Tom and Lucas. "I will be returning to the Saint Clement Danes area tonight. May I take you home?"

Tom nodded. "Yes, please. You're Agent Louvel, Widow Louvel's granddaughter, aren't you?"

"Yes. I'll be leaving shortly," I said, glancing back at Edwin, who was joking with the queen.

I turned to Lucas. "And you?"

He gazed at Bunny. "Her Majesty offered us work here. I think I'll…I think we'll stay. Never thought I'd get to work at the palace. How can you say no to that?"

I smiled at him. "I'll inform Pastor Rosenberry," I said, secretly delighting in anticipation of the Pastor's shocked expression. "Tom, I'll be leaving in a moment."

The boy nodded.

Queen Victoria left Edwin to make her rounds about the room. I rejoined Edwin. "I need to take Tom back to Saint Clement Danes. Since my grand-mère lives close by, I thought… Well, it's Christmas, and she is alone."

Edwin shifted. "Oh. Yes. Well, it's very late. I am sure she's worried about you. And young Tom must be exhausted."

"Yes. Well, I wanted to mention… My offer of dinner stands, if you'd still like to come."

Edwin looked down at me, his eyes soft. He smiled gently. "I'd like that very much."

Hell's bells. I'd nearly forgotten. "I must warn you, my grand-mère is under the impression that you and I are very close to being affianced and that you're desperately in love with me."

Edwin smirked, raising an eyebrow. "Is she?"

I felt my cheeks redden. "A simple misunderstanding."

"I shall do my best to humor her."

I smiled. "I'll see you later tonight then."

Considering it was not long after midnight, tonight was accurate even if it was still dark outside.

He nodded. "Be safe."

"You too."

Leaving Edwin, I went to the queen and princess. "I beg your pardon, Your Majesty. I'll return Tom to Saint Clement Danes and retire for the evening."

Queen Victoria nodded. "You are commended for your service, Agent. I cannot thank you enough."

"You are very welcome, Your Majesty."

The princess stepped forward and curtsied to me. "Thank you, Agent. I can see what you risked for me, for all of us. Thank you."

I smiled at her then curtsied. "You're very welcome, Princess."

The child nodded to me then turned back to the others.

I grinned at Victoria, whose eyes delighted in the small change—at least for tonight—in her child.

Waving to Tom, I motioned it was time to leave.

I cast one last look back at Edwin, who stood by the fire. My heart ached to leave him there. But there was still Grand-mère to contend with, and keeping her enthusiasm for my fictionalized version of Edwin was going to be more challenging to manage than taking down Krampus.

CHAPTER 22
Under the Mistletoe

"Oranges and lemons, you scared me half to death," Grand-mère said as she unbolted the door. "Do you know what time it is?"

"Almost four, I think. I'm very sorry. I've just finished a case," I said with a yawn as I entered.

"A case. The children?"

I nodded.

"Everyone okay?"

"They are now."

"Do you want tea? Let me fix you something to eat."

I shook my head. "Sleep. Want sleep," I said groggily.

Grand-mère laughed. "Clemeny," she said with a shake of the head. "Why I ever let Eliza talk me into letting you go is beyond me. Your bed is made, my girl. I was expecting you."

Yawning once more, I kissed her on the cheek. I was about to head to bed but paused first. Stopping at the hearth, I pulled a sprig of mistletoe from my pocket and lay it on the mantelpiece.

"What is that leaf?"

"Mistletoe."

"And why do we have that there?"

"Because Queen Victoria said so."

Grand-mère chuckled.

"Make sure you don't move it," I said. "Promise. No cleaning it up."

"I promise. Now go sleep. We'll have a big breakfast in the morning then get ready for Christmas dinner. Is your gentleman caller still coming?"

Gentleman caller. "Yes," I said, this time answering honestly.

"Very good. Goodnight, my love," she chirped happily, waving me off to bed.

I ambled to my small room and slumped into my bed. I heard Grand-mère's bed creak as she slipped into her own bed once more as well. Soon, everything fell silent. Just before my eyes closed, I looked out the window. Fat snowflakes were falling. They shimmered in the glow of the moonlight. Now, all was calm. Now, all was bright. Not a creature was stirring. And I fell fast asleep for the night knowing that Krampus was back in the Otherworld where he belonged. And that Edwin Hunter was coming to dinner.

The flat smelled of roasted ham with spiced apples, turnips, and freshly baked bread. A beautifully decorated Bûche de Noël sat on the middle of the table. The thick dark chocolate frosting and black cherries seemed to call out my name. If Edwin didn't come soon, I wasn't sure I was going to be able to resist.

Grand-mère was about to ask me for the hundredth time when my guest would arrive when there was a knock on the door.

"I will answer," Grand-mère said then rose. A second later, she shook her head. "No. You must answer. Be all feminine politeness. Curtsey like this," she said, inclining her head so her neck appeared long, her profile gentled.

I rolled my eyes at her. She had already talked me into wearing a green holiday gown, my hair tied up with a sprig of holly. I felt like I'd gone back to my younger years before I'd swapped the confines of a corset for my trousers and vambraces.

"Fine," I said, rising. "But I'm not doing that."

Grand-mère rolled her eyes then muttered in French.

"I can hear you. And it's Christmas."

"Yes, yes," she said, shooing me off.

I went to the door and took a deep breath. Opening the door, I found Edwin standing there with a light dusting of snow on his shoulders.

"Happy Christmas," I said.

He stared at me.

"Edwin?"

"Sorry. It's just…Happy Christmas," he said then smiled gently at me. "You look beautiful."

A flash of heat rose in my cheeks. "Thank you."

I stepped back so he could enter and helped him shrug out of his coat which I hung on the coat stand.

"Come in, come in, come in," Grand-mère called. Apparently, she'd held herself back to give us a moment, but could wait no longer.

I held my breath.

"So, you are Agent Hunter. Oh, oranges and lemons, a fine cut of a gentleman. Eliza was right. Do come in. How about a wassail? It's very cold outside. Come, come. Clemeny, sit Agent Hunter down by the hearth so he can warm up. Dinner will be served within the hour. It's a pleasure to meet you. I am Felice Louvel, Clemeny's grand-mère. I have heard so much about you. Now, let me bring you some wine. Sit, sit."

I nodded to Edwin, who followed me to the small parlor. While the flat was tiny, Grand-mère had decorated it nicely for the holiday. The fire burned cheerfully, filling the room with an orange glow.

Edwin walked over to the fireplace. Chuckling, he lifted the spring of mistletoe. "From the palace?"

I nodded then joined him. "It seemed prudent. How are the children?"

"Remarkably resilient and recovering very well. Mister Anderson and the Browns asked me to send my thanks."

I smiled. "And Her Majesty and the princess?"

"Well, the princess's manners are in check, for now. Perhaps we should have let Krampus stay a bit longer just to be sure."

I grinned. "Be careful. Wicked talk might just summon him back."

Edwin twirled the sprig of mistletoe between his fingers. "I think I'm safe. As will everyone else be once the kissing fashion takes hold."

A heavy silence fell between us.

After a moment, Edwin stepped closer to me. He studied my face carefully. Reaching out, he gently removed the black silk eye patch I was wearing. He set it on the mantel then turned and smiled gently at me.

"Clemeny, I…I'm not sure I can be your reporting director anymore," he said.

Well, that was unexpected. "Why not?"

"Because there is a new law."

"A new law?"

"You see, I may request a kiss from the girl I fancy in the presence of mistletoe. It would be improper for me to kiss a subordinate. But…but I can kiss the girl I favor."

"Then kiss me, Edwin."

He leaned in and set the most gentle of kisses on my lips. And, as I had long imagined, his soft, warm kiss tasted slightly salty and of spicy-sweet cinnamon. And in that moment, I realized I had never, ever, had a merrier Christmas.

Continue Clemeny's Adventures in Bitches and Brawlers

BITCHES
AND
BRAWLERS
A RED RIDING HOOD RETELLING
MELANIE KARSAK
NEW YORK TIMES BESTSELLING AUTHOR

About the Author

New York Times and *USA Today* bestselling author Melanie Karsak is the author of *The Celtic Blood Series, The Road to Valhalla Series, The Celtic Rebels Series, Steampunk Fairy Tales* and many more works of fiction. The author currently lives in Florida with her husband and two children.

- amazon.com/author/melaniekarsak
- facebook.com/authormelaniekarsak
- instagram.com/karsakmelanie
- pinterest.com/melaniekarsak
- bookbub.com/authors/melanie-karsak
- youtube.com/@authormelaniekarsak

Also by Melanie Karsak

THE CELTIC BLOOD SERIES:

Highland Raven

Highland Blood

Highland Vengeance

Highland Queen

THE CELTIC REBELS SERIES:

Queen of Oak: A Novel of Boudica

Queen of Stone: A Novel of Boudica

Queen of Ash and Iron: A Novel of Boudica

THE ROAD TO VALHALLA SERIES:

Under the Strawberry Moon

Shield-Maiden: Under the Howling Moon

Shield-Maiden: Under the Hunter's Moon

Shield-Maiden: Under the Thunder Moon

Shield-Maiden: Under the Blood Moon

Shield-Maiden: Under the Dark Moon

THE SHADOWS OF VALHALLA SERIES:

Shield-Maiden: Winternights Gambit

Shield-Maiden: Gambit of Blood

Shield-Maiden: Gambit of Shadows

Shield-Maiden: Gambit of Swords

Eagles and Crows

The Blackthorn Queen

The Crow Queen

THE HARVESTING SERIES:

The Harvesting

Midway

The Shadow Aspect

Witch Wood

The Torn World

STEAMPUNK FAIRY TALES:

Curiouser and Curiouser: Steampunk Alice in Wonderland

Ice and Embers: Steampunk Snow Queen

Beauty and Beastly: Steampunk Beauty and the Beast

Golden Braids and Dragon Blades: Steampunk Rapunzel

THE RED CAPE SOCIETY

Wolves and Daggers

Alphas and Airships

Peppermint and Pentacles

Bitches and Brawlers

Howls and Hallows

Lycans and Legends

THE AIRSHIP RACING CHRONICLES:

Chasing the Star Garden

Chasing the Green Fairy

Chasing Christmas Past

THE CHANCELLOR FAIRY TALES:

The Glass Mermaid

The Cupcake Witch

The Fairy Godfather

The Vintage Medium

The Book Witch

        Find these books and more on Amazon!

Printed in Great Britain
by Amazon